Abracadabra STRINGS

BOOK 1

PIANO ACCOMPANIMENTS

Arrangements by Christopher Hussey and Jane Sebba

To accompany the new fully revised and expanded
Abracadabra Violin, Viola and Cello.

A & C Black · London

CONTENTS

1. Pizz on D
2. Pizz A pizza!
3. Bobby Shafto
4. When the saints go marching in
5. Supercalifragilistic-expialidocious
6. A tisket, a tasket
7. Little playmates
8. Mobile phone
9. Fiddle fanfare
10. A friend in DEED
11. One finger dance
12. Eee-abba-dabba-dee!
13. Spinning wheel
14. A stitch in time
15. Frère Jacques
16. Welsh lullaby (Suo-gân)
17. Windmill song
18. Hot cross buns
19. Merrily we roll along
20. Pease pudding hot
21. Clown dance
22. Road monsters
23. Au clair de la lune
24. Twinkle, twinkle little bow
25. Miss Mary Mac
26. The song that never stops
27. Whistle while you work
28. Secret agents
29. Little bird
30. Summer shine
31. Halfway down the stairs
32. Old MacDonald
33. Brown bread
34. Big Ben
35. Turn the glasses over (a round)
36. Off to France in the morning
37. Racing driver (a round)
38. Long, long ago
39. Ode to joy
40. The way you look tonight
41. (Meet the) Flintstones
42. I came from Alabama
43. Morningtown ride
44. Troika
45. Daydreamer
46. Roses from the South
47. Lavender's blue
48. Call of the carousel
49. We all stand together
50. Edelweiss
51. On top of Old Smokey
52. London's burning (a round)
53. The hippopotamus song
54. London Bridge
55. Tea for two
56. Stand by me
57. Skye boat song
58. Jupiter
59. Feed the birds
60. Kalinka
61. The old bazaar in Cairo
62. Muck! (a round)
63. Waltz

64 Puff the magic dragon	78 EastEnders
65 Dumplins	79 Happy birthday
66 Row, row, row your boat (a round)	80 Heigh-ho
	81 The Addams family
67 Pop! goes the weasel	82 The mocking bird
68 Dance of the cuckoos	83 Chim chim cher-ee
69 The shepherdess (a round)	84 Ragamuffin's rag
70 We're off to see the Wizard	85 Who will buy?
71 Egyptian snake dance	86 Beauty and the Beast
72 Shalom (a round)	87 Barcarolle
73 Summer is icumen in (a round)	88 Millennium
74 Part of your world	89 Watch out kookaburra! (a round)
75 Short'nin' bread	90 Nocturne
76 What shall we do with the drunken sailor?	Acknowledgements
77 Winter wonderland	Index

A&C Black Publishers Ltd
37 Soho Square, London W1D 3QZ
© 2002 A&C Black Publishers Ltd

ISBN 0 7136 6314 6

Illustrations by Paul Parks
Cover illustration by Dee Shulman
Design by Jocelyn Lucas
Music setting by Christopher Hussey and Jeanne Fisher
Edited by Carla Moss and Jane Sebba

Photocopying prohibited

All rights reserved. No part of this publication may be reproduced in any form or by any means — photographic, electronic or mechanical, including photocopying, recording, taping or information storage and retrieval systems — without the prior permission in writing of the publishers.

A&C Black uses paper produced with elemental chlorine-free pulp, harvested from managed sustainable forests.

Printed by Caligraving Ltd, Thetford, Norfolk

1 Pizz on D

CH/VSP

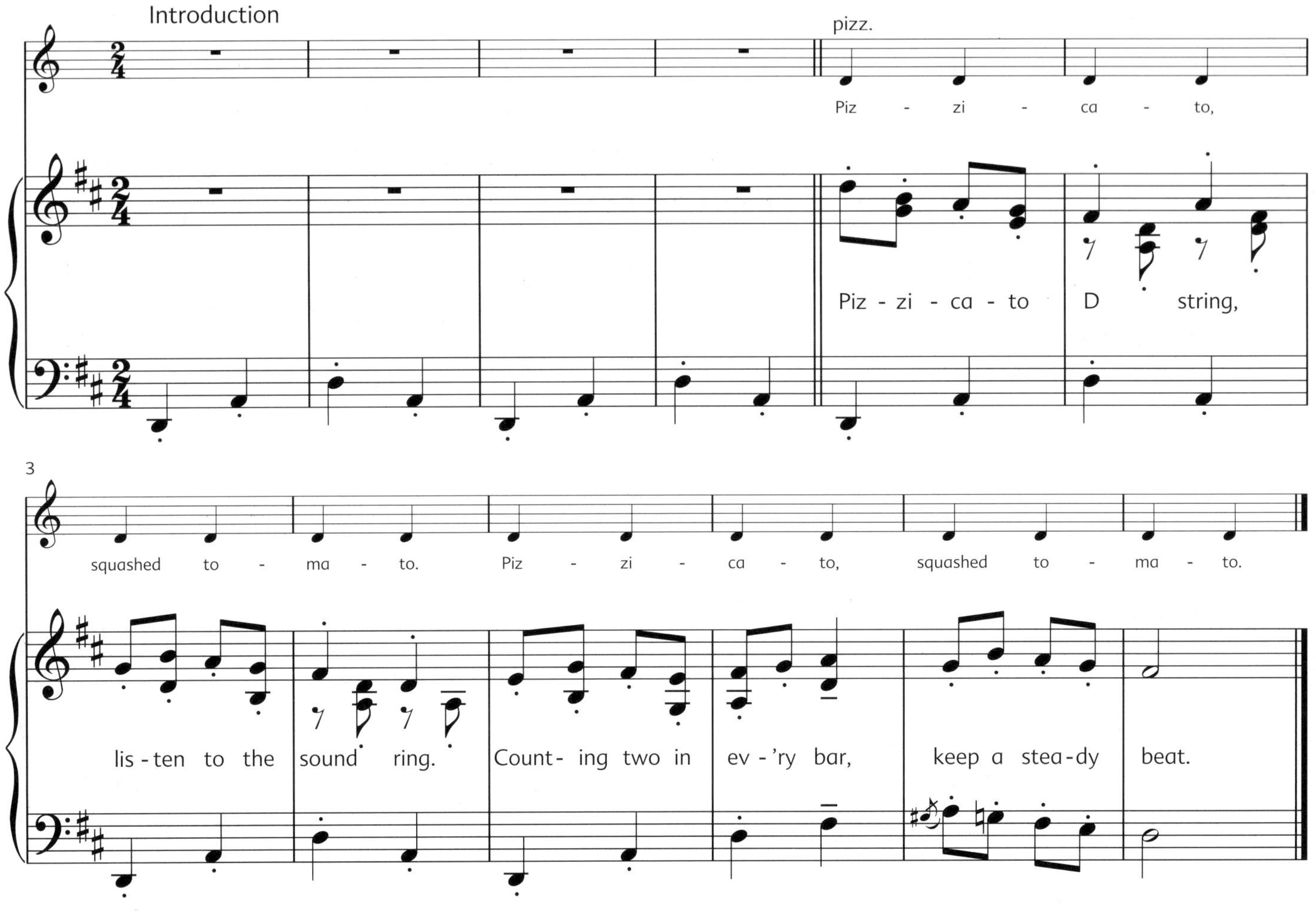
Introduction
pizz.
Piz - zi - ca - to,
Piz - zi - ca - to D string,
3
squashed to - ma - to. Piz - zi - ca - to, squashed to - ma - to.
lis - ten to the sound ring. Count- ing two in ev - 'ry bar, keep a stea - dy beat.

2 Pizz A pizza!

CH/JS

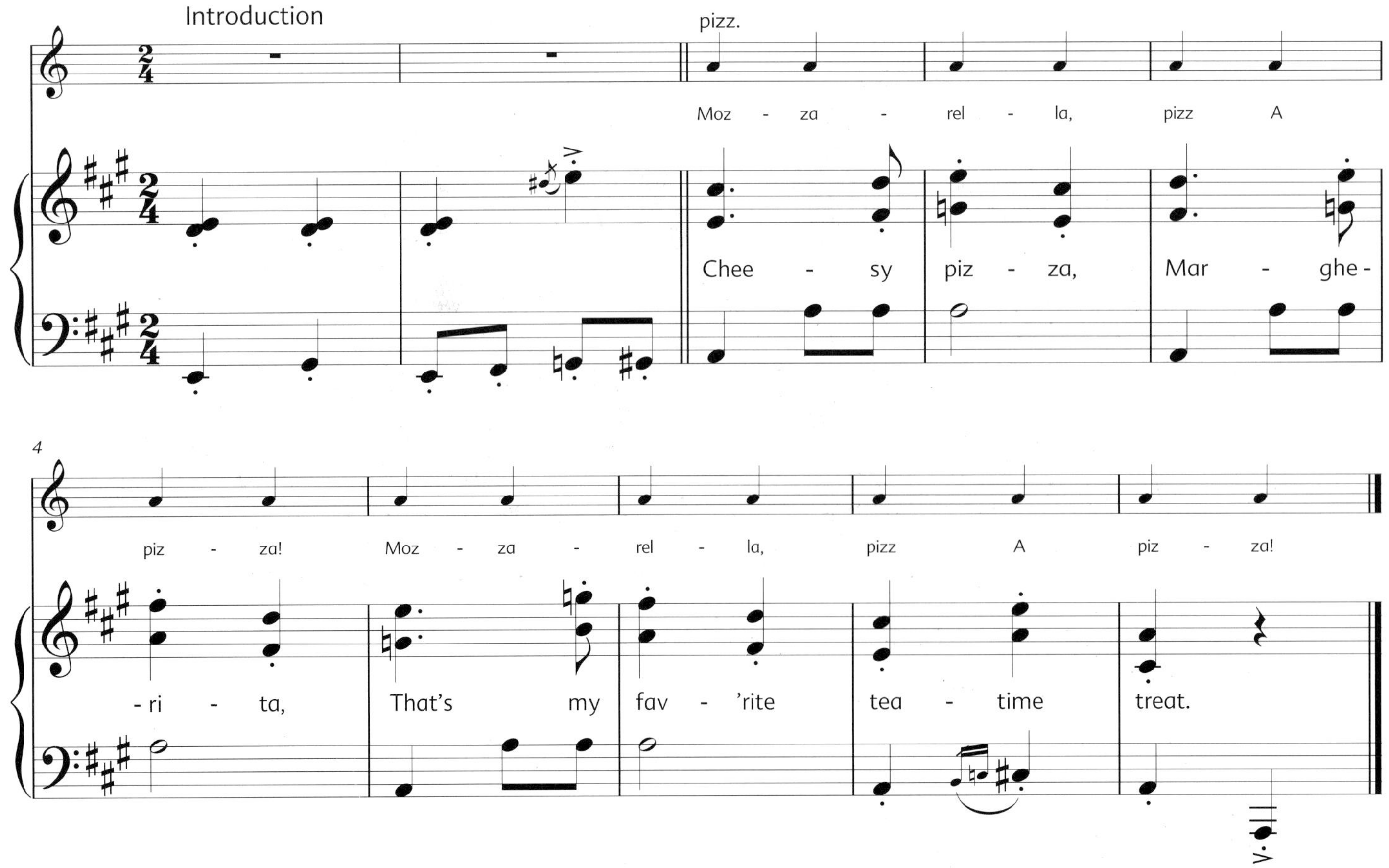
Introduction
pizz.
Moz - za - rel - la, pizz A
Chee - sy piz - za, Mar - ghe -
4
piz - za! Moz - za - rel - la, pizz A piz - za!
- ri - ta, That's my fav - 'rite tea - time treat.

3 Bobby Shafto

traditional

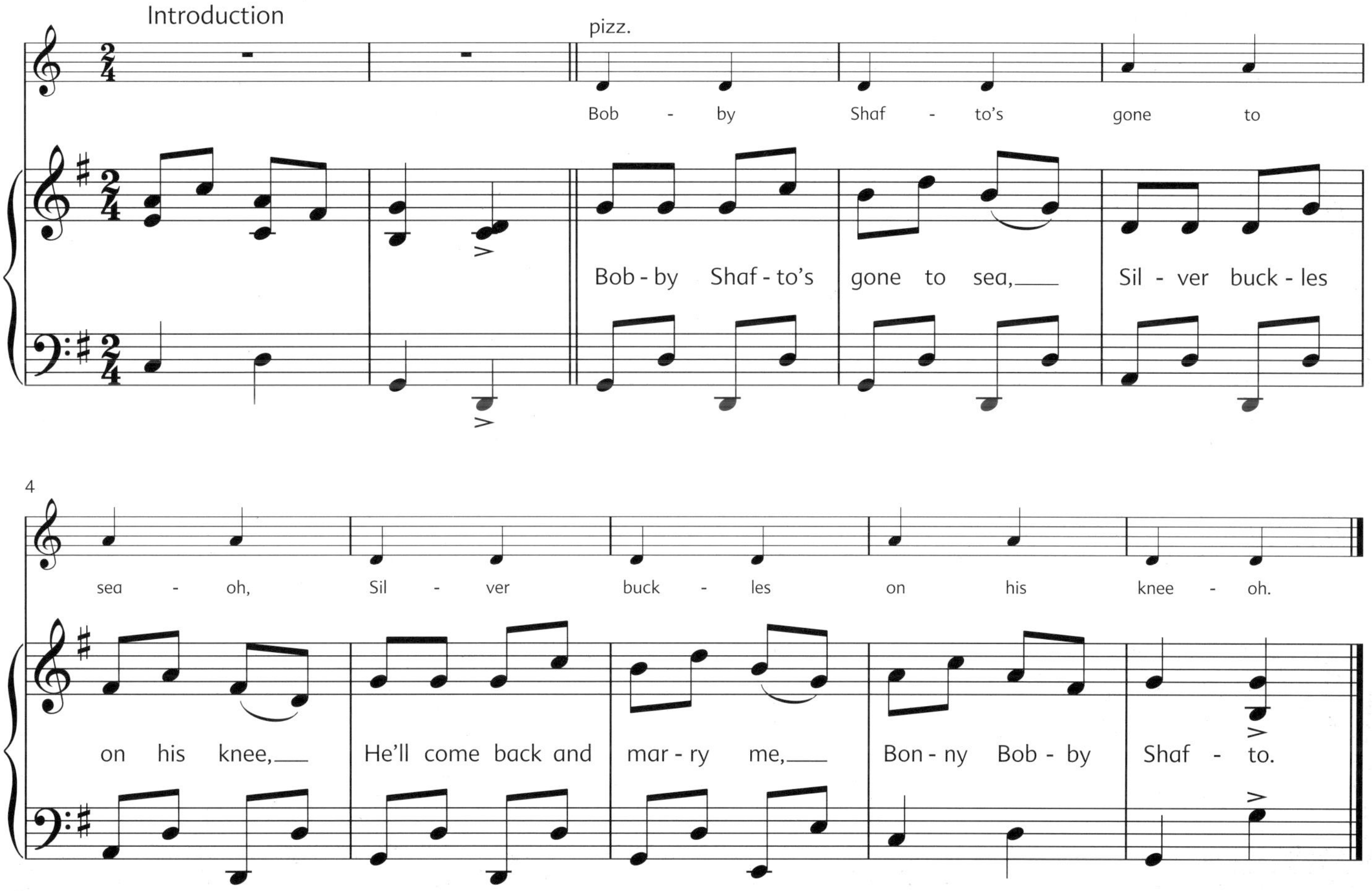
Introduction
pizz.
Bob - by Shaf - to's gone to
Bob - by Shaf - to's gone to sea, Sil - ver buck - les
4
sea - oh, Sil - ver buck - les on his knee - oh.
on his knee, He'll come back and mar - ry me, Bon - ny Bob - by Shaf - to.

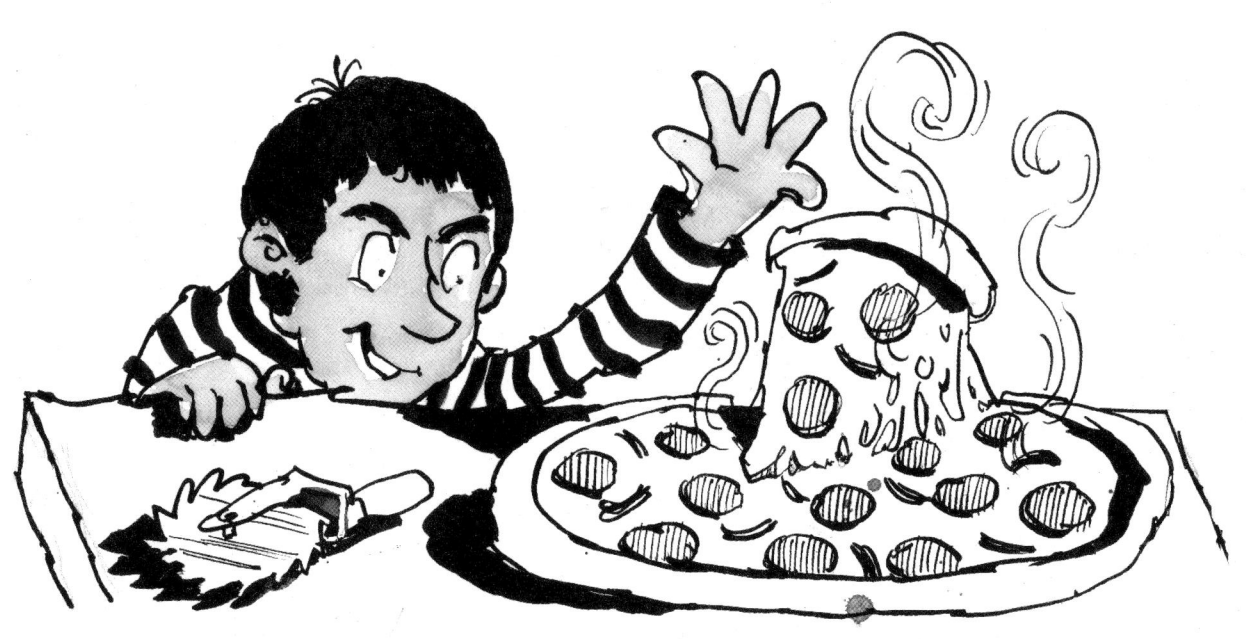

5 Supercalifragilisticexpialidocious

Richard M Sherman and Robert B Sherman

6 A-tisket, a-tasket

words CH, music traditional

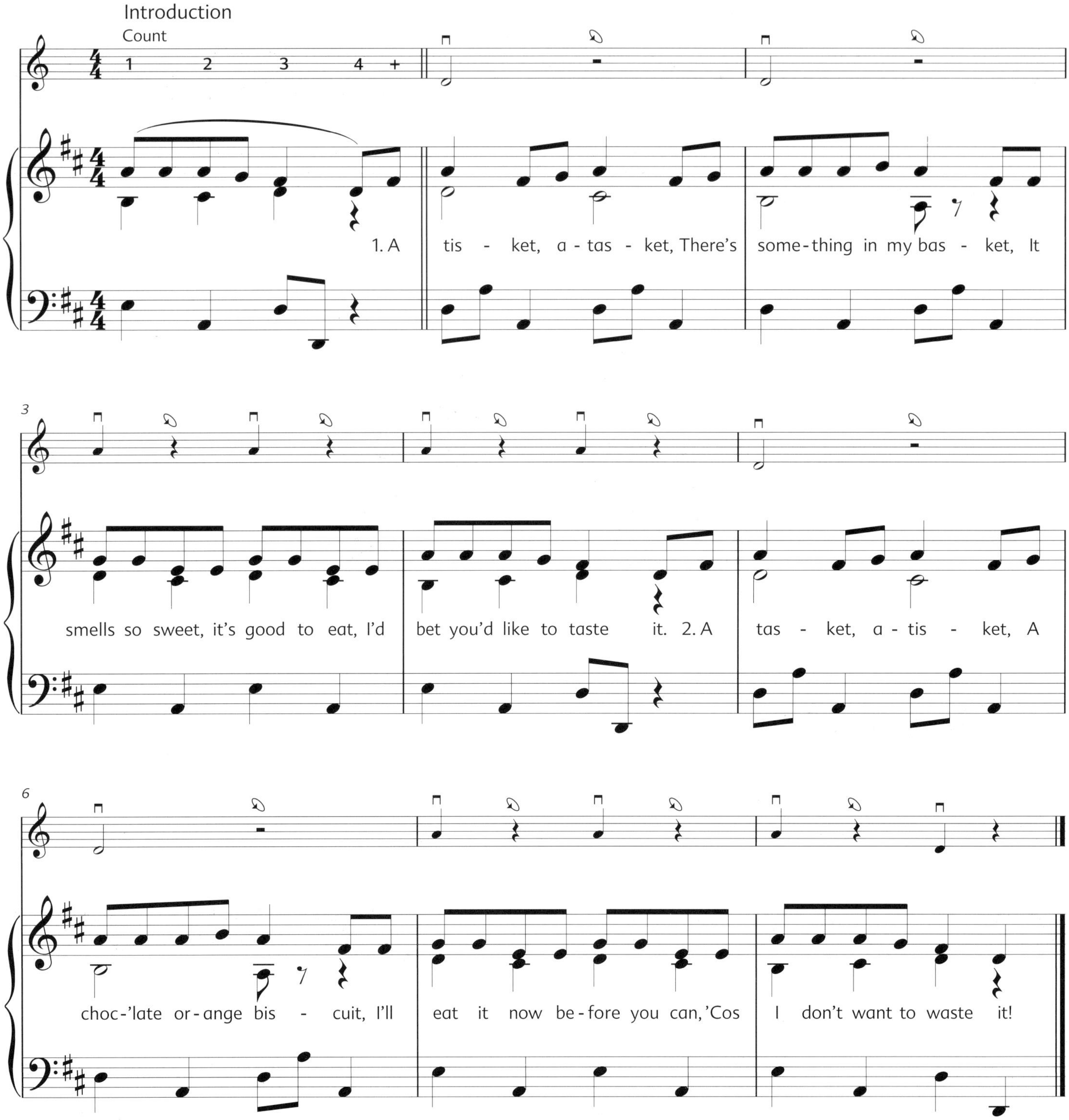
Introduction
Count
1 2 3 4 +
1. A tis - ket, a - tas - ket, There's some-thing in my bas - ket, It
smells so sweet, it's good to eat, I'd bet you'd like to taste it. 2. A tas - ket, a - tis - ket, A
choc-'late or-ange bis - cuit, I'll eat it now be-fore you can, 'Cos I don't want to waste it!

7 Little playmates

F X Chwatal

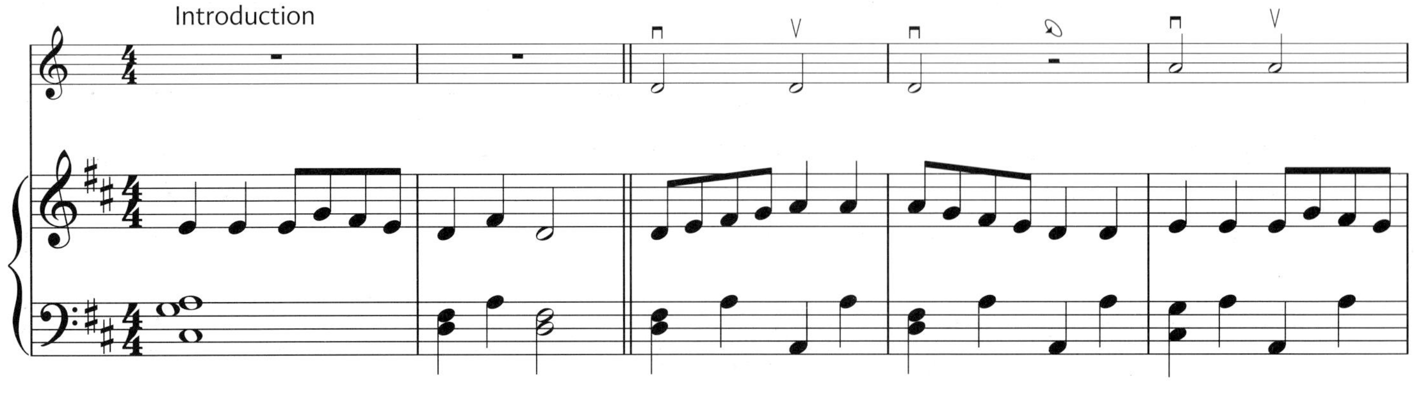
Introduction

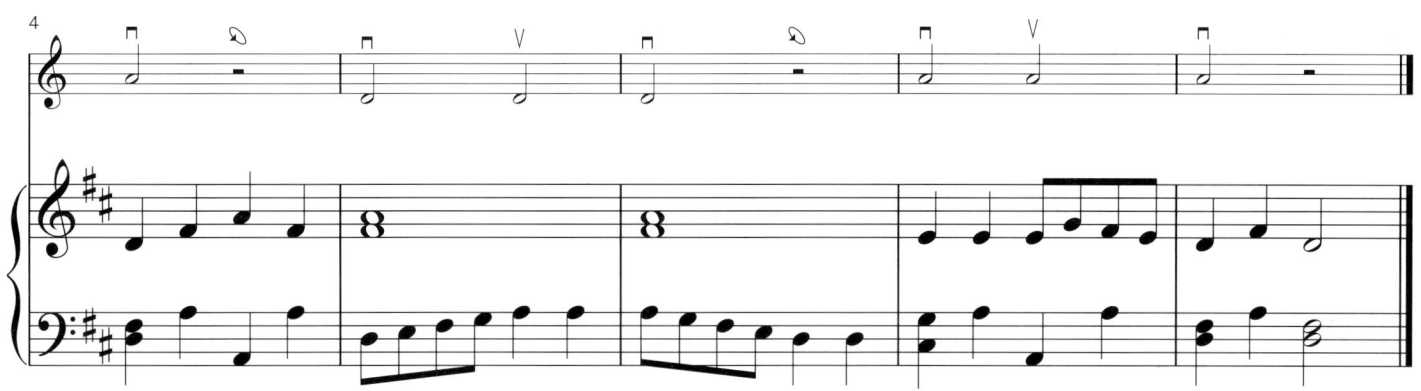

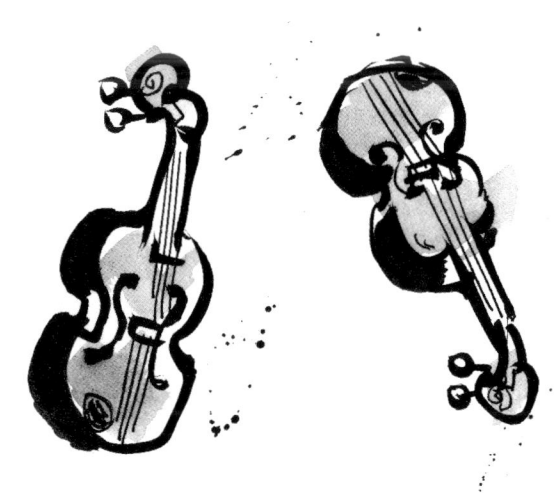

8 Mobile phone

words JS, music traditional

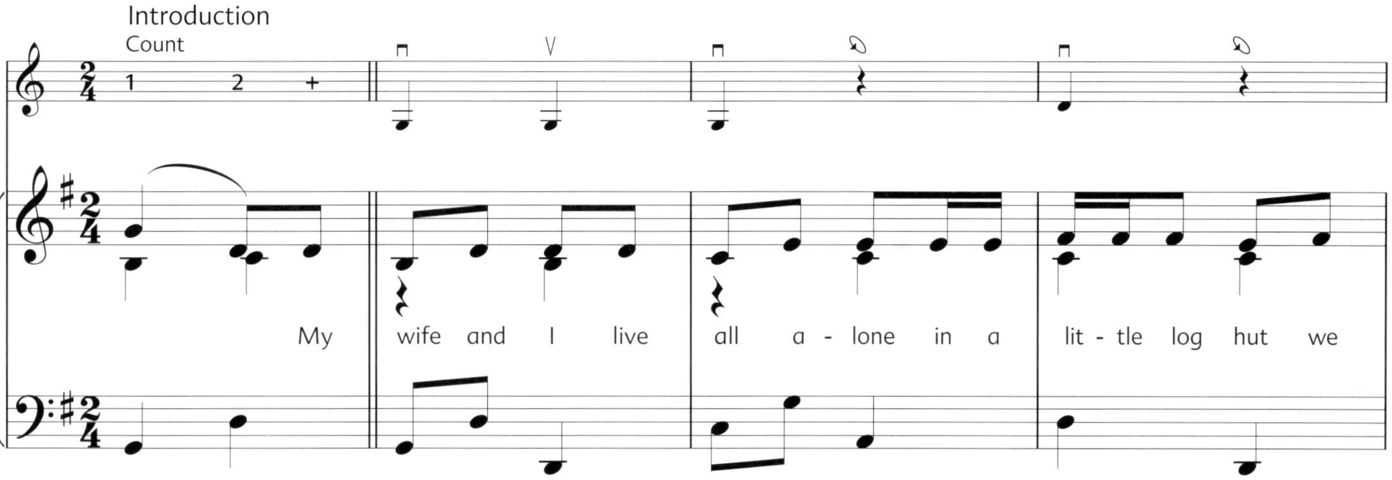
Introduction
Count
1 2 +
My wife and I live all a - lone in a lit - tle log hut we

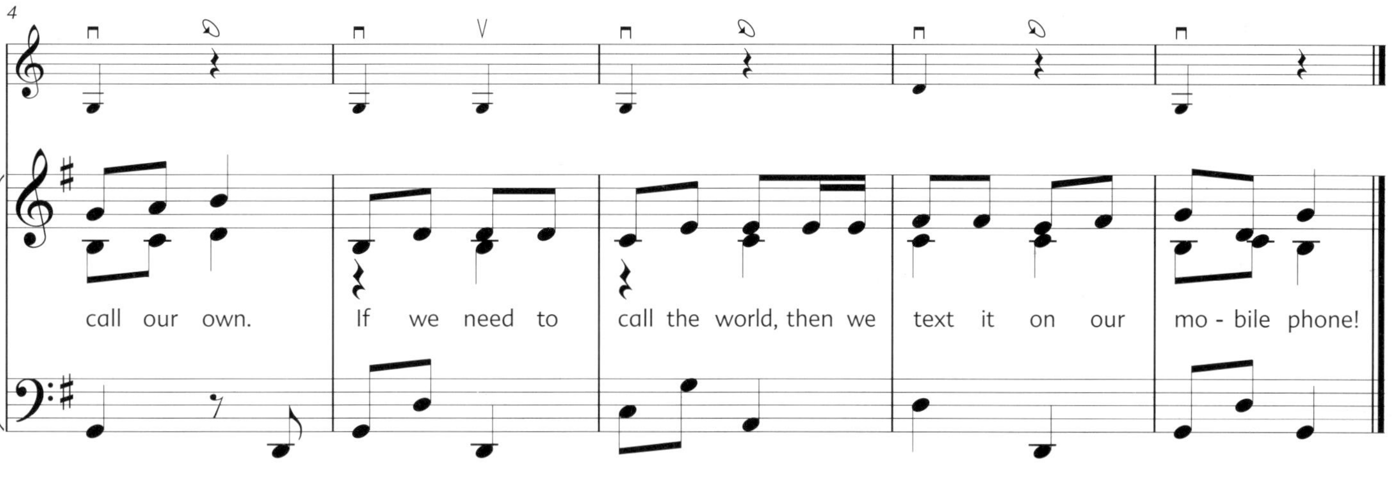
call our own. If we need to call the world, then we text it on our mo - bile phone!

9 Fiddle fanfare

CH

10 A friend in DEED

11 One finger dance
PD

12 Eee-abba-dabba-dee!

CH

Lyrics: E A B B A, D A B B A, D E E, Fred and me, Eee - ab - ba - dab - ba - dee!

13 Spinning wheel / 14 A stitch in time

PD/CH

15 Frère Jacques

traditional French

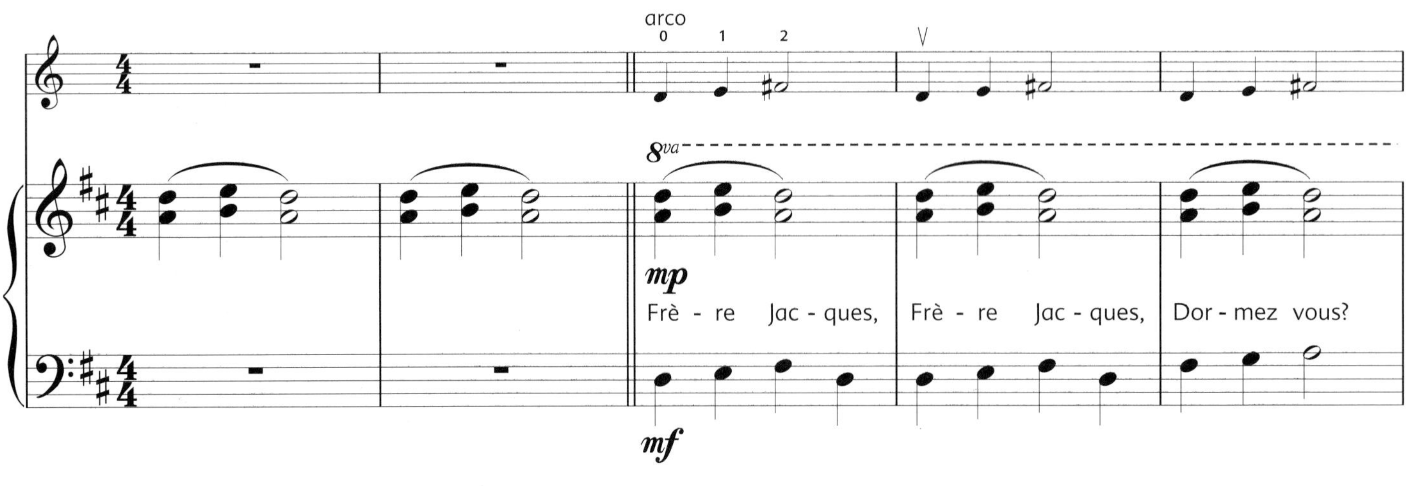

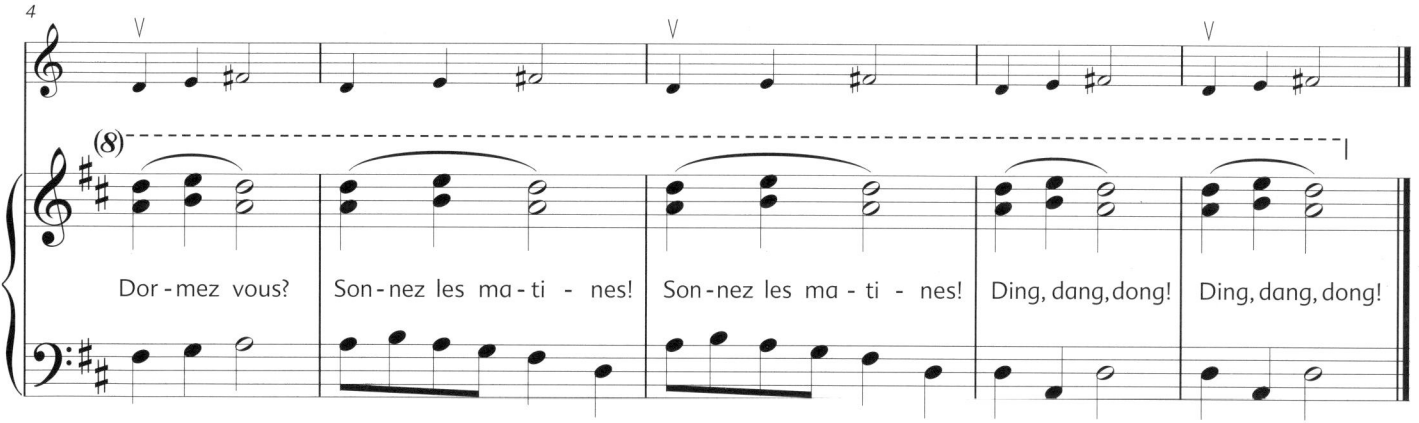

16 Welsh lullaby (Suo-gân)

traditional Welsh

17 Windmill song

words CH, music PD

Sails go round, the corn is ground for flour in-side the wind - mill. wind - mill.

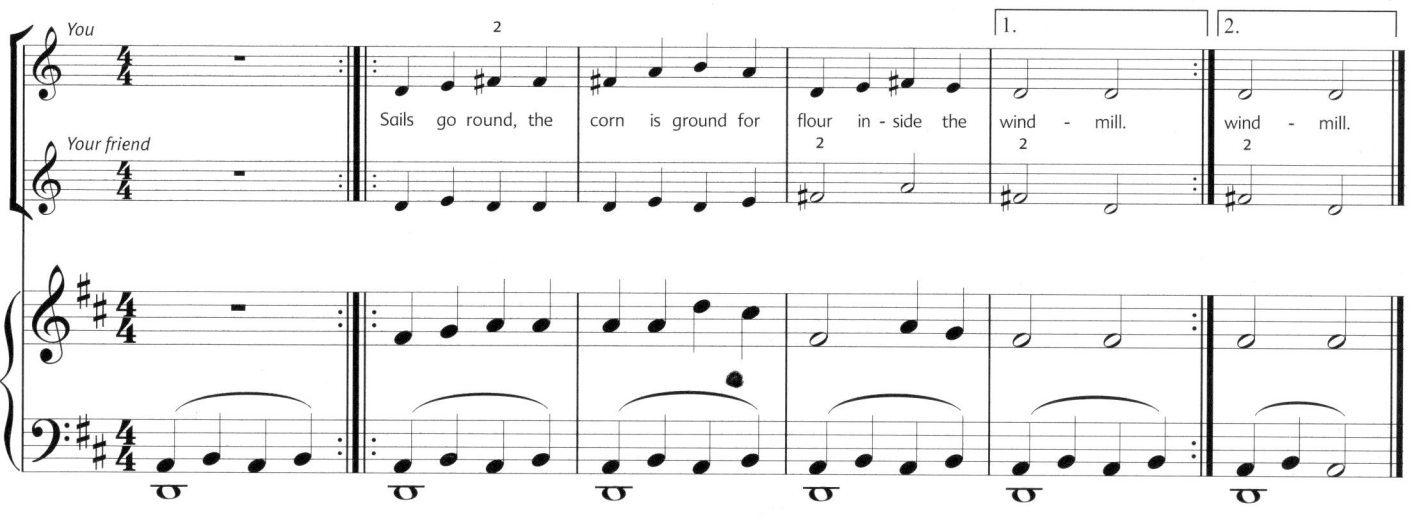

18 Hot cross buns

traditional

Hot cross buns, hot cross buns, One a penny, two a penny, hot cross buns.

19 Merrily we roll along

traditional

20 Pease pudding hot

traditional

Pease pud-ding hot, pease pud-ding cold. Pease pud-ding in the pot grow-ing mould!

21 Clown dance

traditional French

Fine
D.S. al Fine

Pupil's part written with D.C. al Fine instead of D.S. al Fine.

24 Twinkle, twinkle little bow

words JS, music traditional

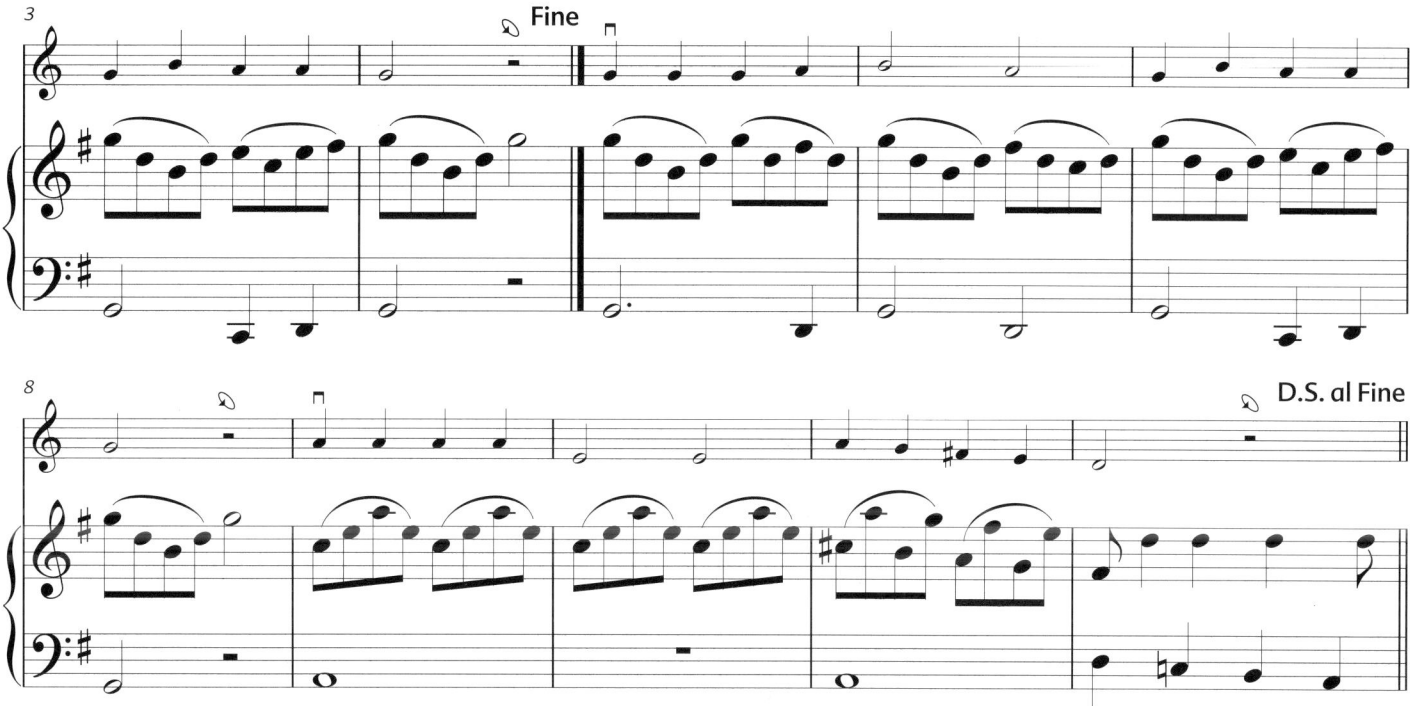

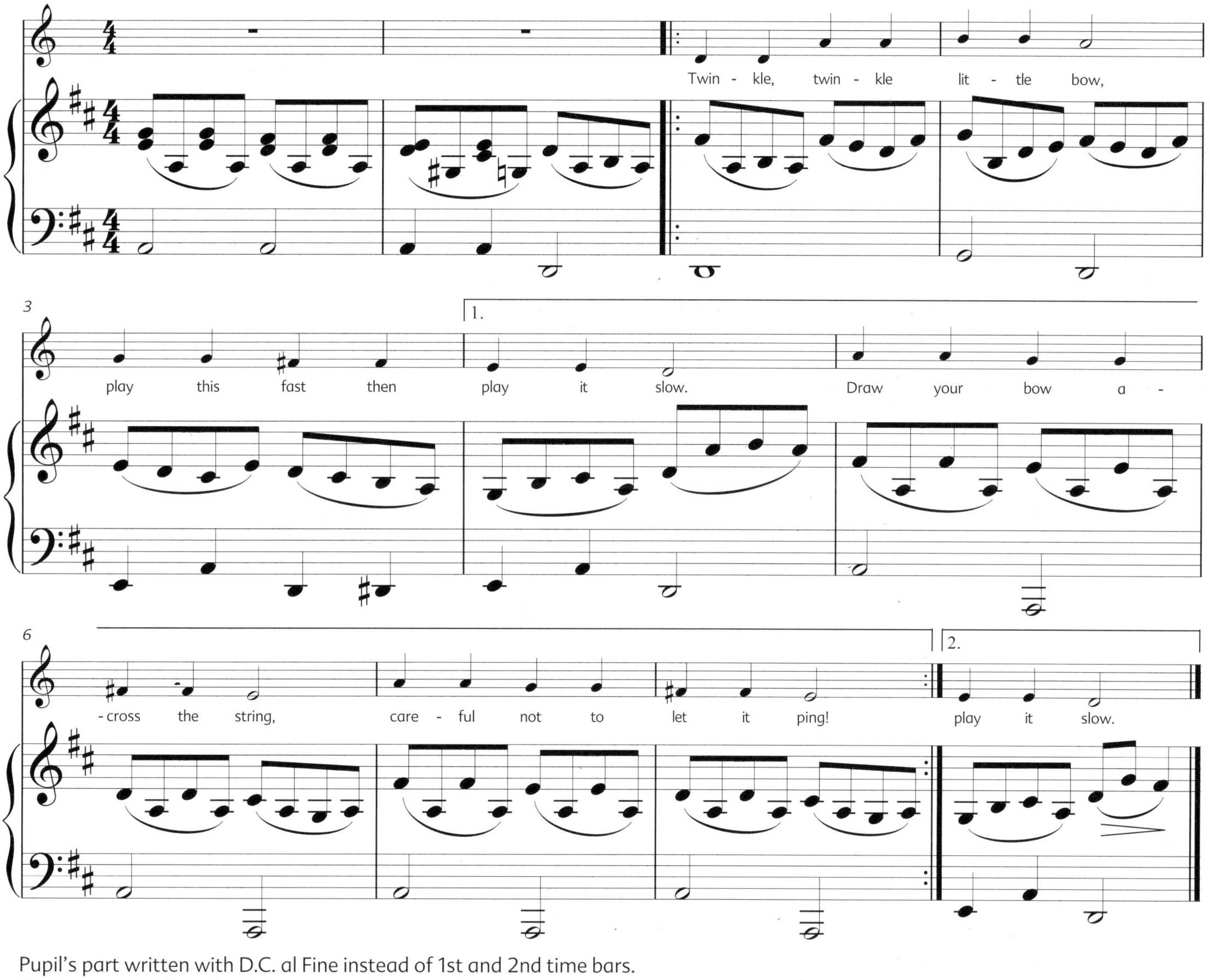
Twin - kle, twin - kle lit - tle bow,
play this fast then play it slow.
Draw your bow a - cross the string, care - ful not to let it ping!
play it slow.

Pupil's part written with D.C. al Fine instead of 1st and 2nd time bars.
Omit piano RH if teacher's instrumental part is played.

26 The song that never stops

CH

This song can start and nev-er stop, You'll keep on play-ing 'til you drop! This 'til you drop!

Pupil's part written as four bars with repeat.

27 Whistle while you work

words Larry Morey, music Frank Churchill

28 Secret agents

words JS, music traditional

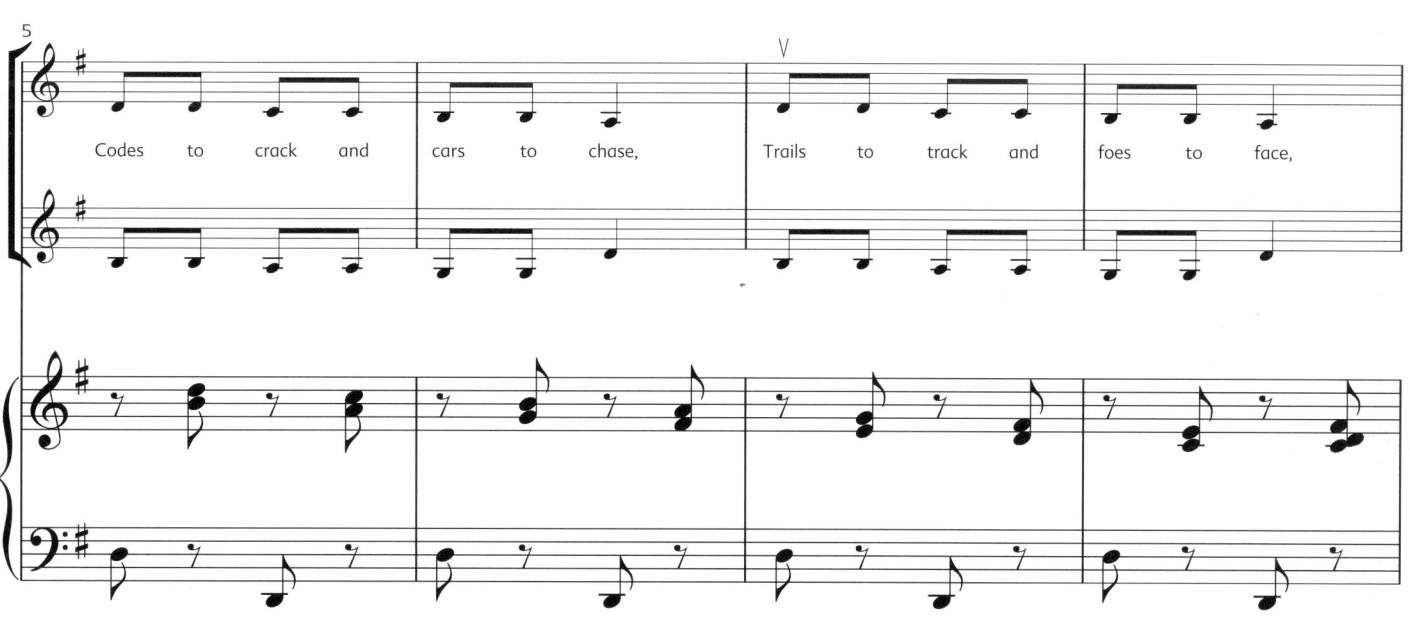

29 Little bird

traditional German

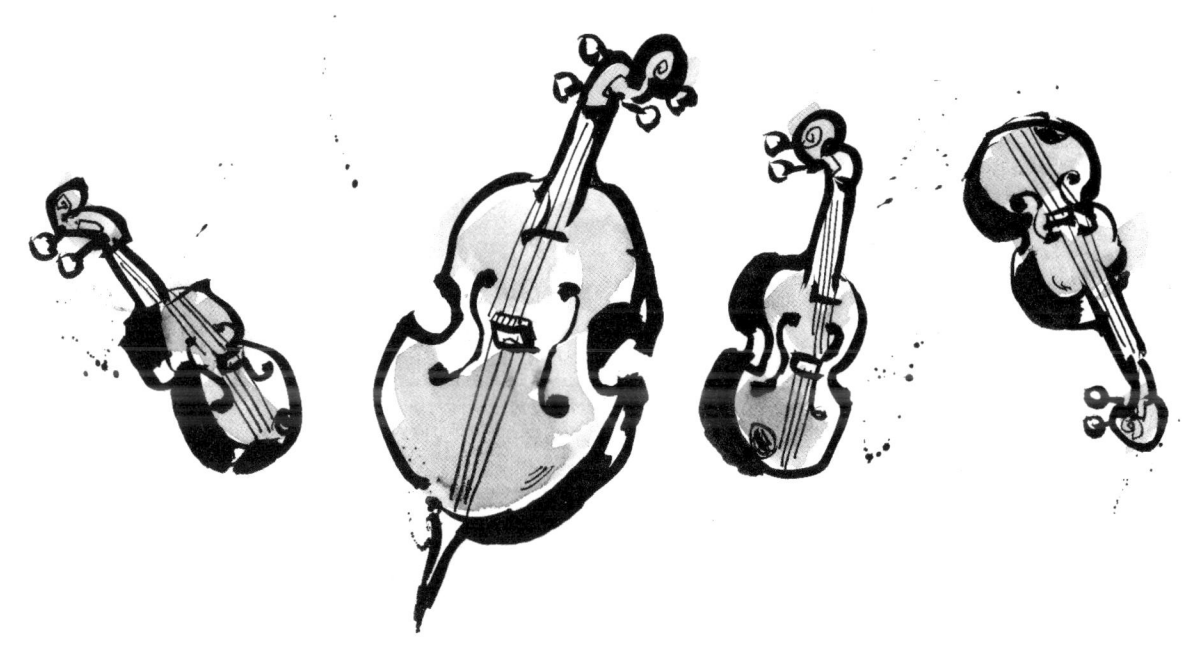

30 Summer shine

words CH, music PD

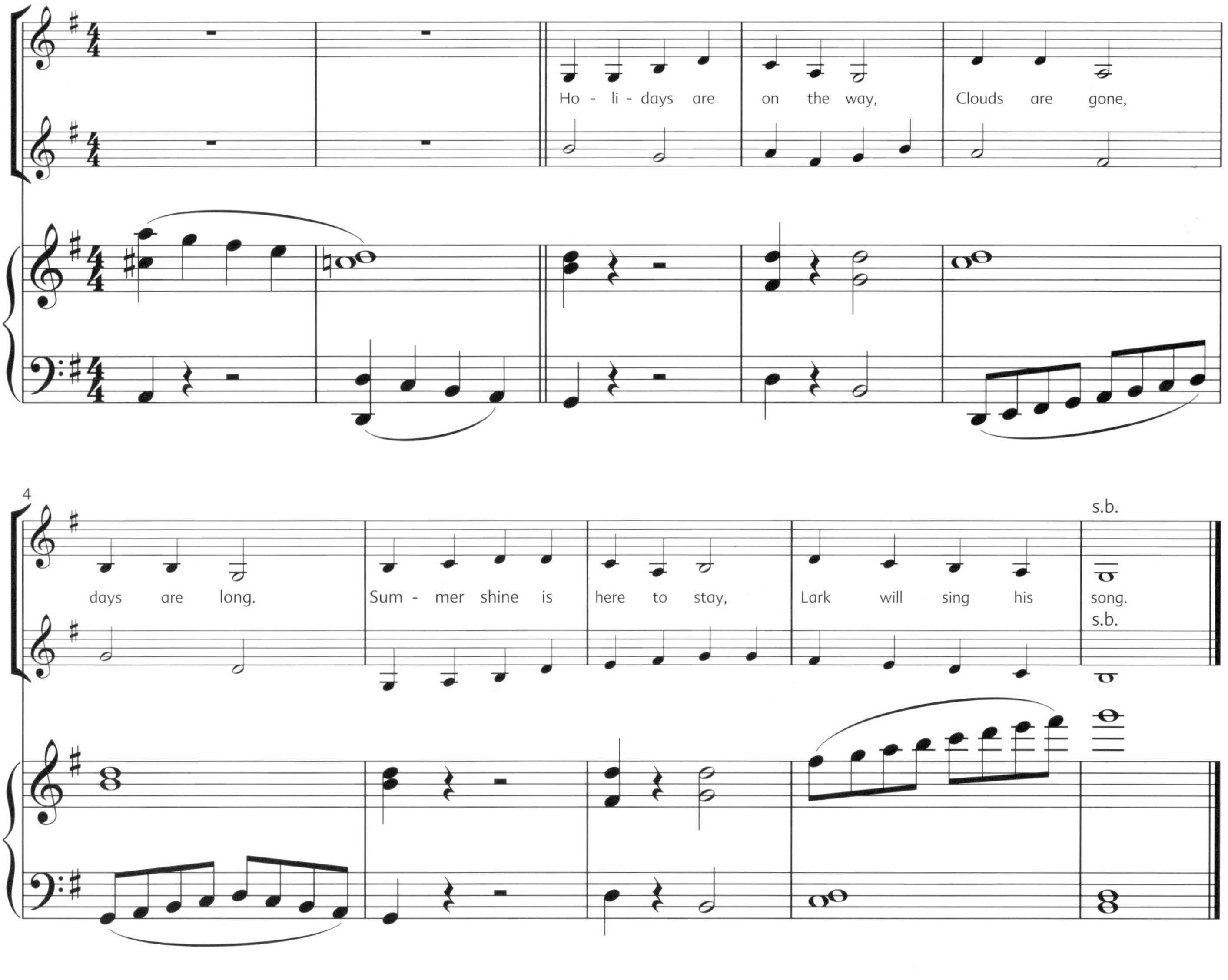
Ho - li - days are on the way,
Clouds are gone,
4
days are long.
Sum - mer shine is here to stay,
Lark will sing his song.
s.b.
s.b.

31 Halfway down the stairs

words A A Milne, music H Fraser Simson

Half-way down the stairs is a stair where I sit: There isn't any o-ther stair that's quite like it. I'm not at the bot-tom and I'm not at the top: So this is the stair where I al-ways stop.

32 Old MacDonald

words adapted by SR, music traditional

33 Brown bread

CH

Pupil's part written with D.C. al Fine instead of D.S. al Fine.

34 Big Ben

35 Turn the glasses over (a round)

traditional

* entry point when played as a round

The accompaniment fits when the piece is played both as a solo and as a round — repeat the last two bars of accompaniment as necessary until the last player has finished.

36 Off to France in the morning

words CH, music PD

37 Racing driver (a round)

words CH, music traditional French

* entry point when played as a round

The accompaniment fits when the piece is played both as a solo and as a round — repeat the last two bars of accompaniment as necessary until the last player has finished.

38 Long, long ago

Thomas H Bayly

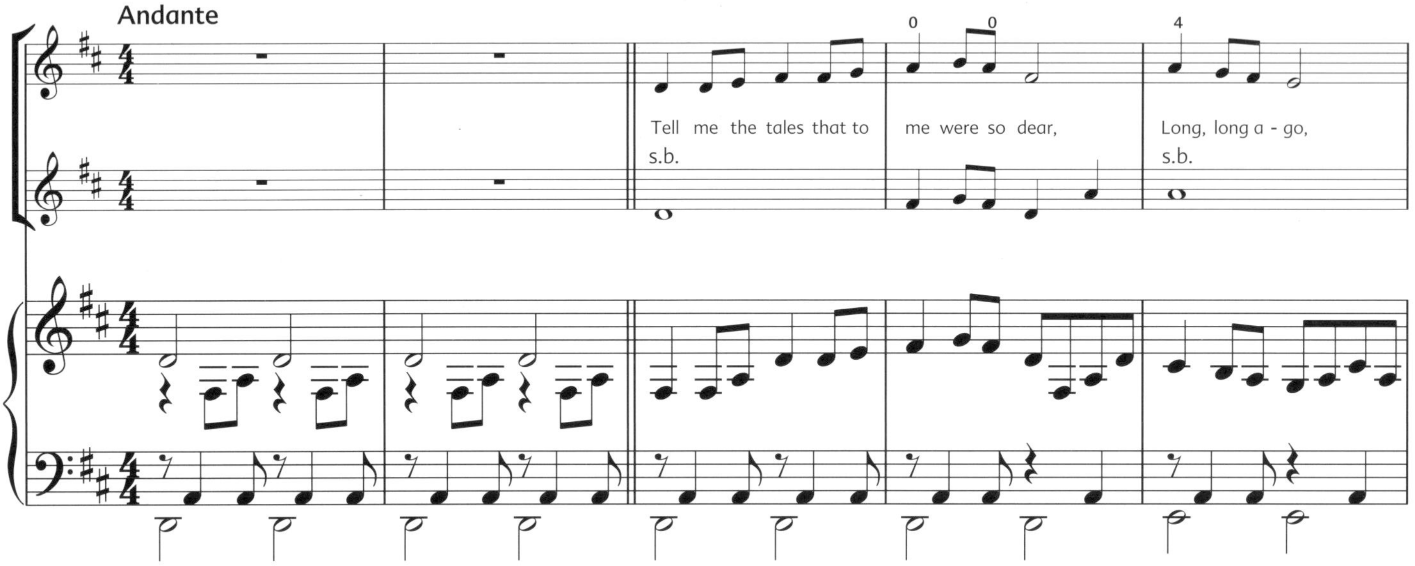

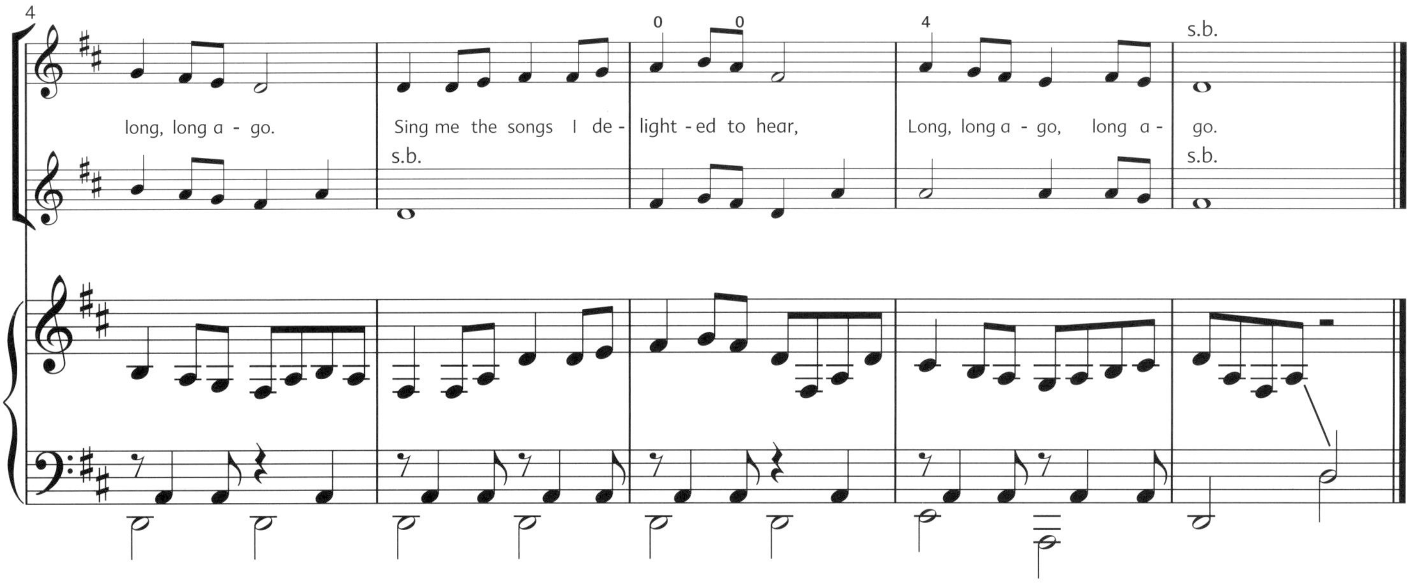

39 Ode to joy

Ludwig van Beethoven

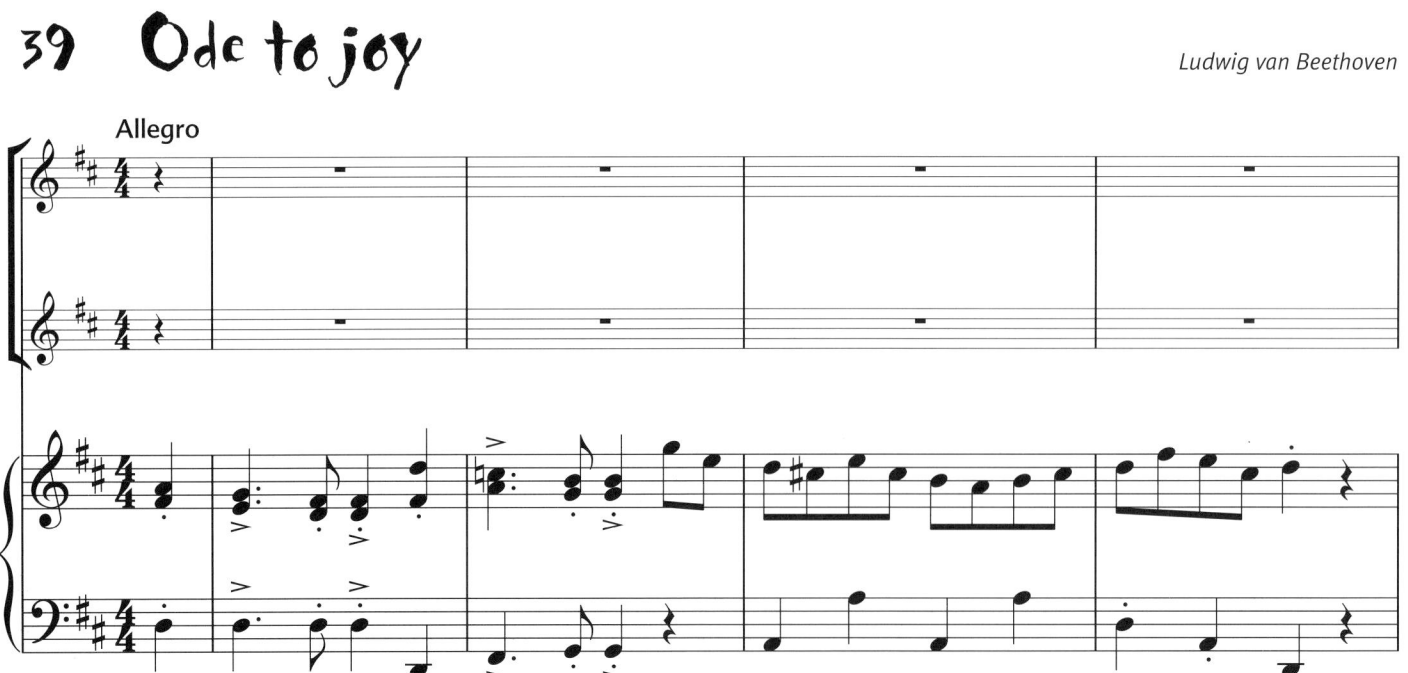

40 The way you look tonight

Jerome Kern

Cantabile

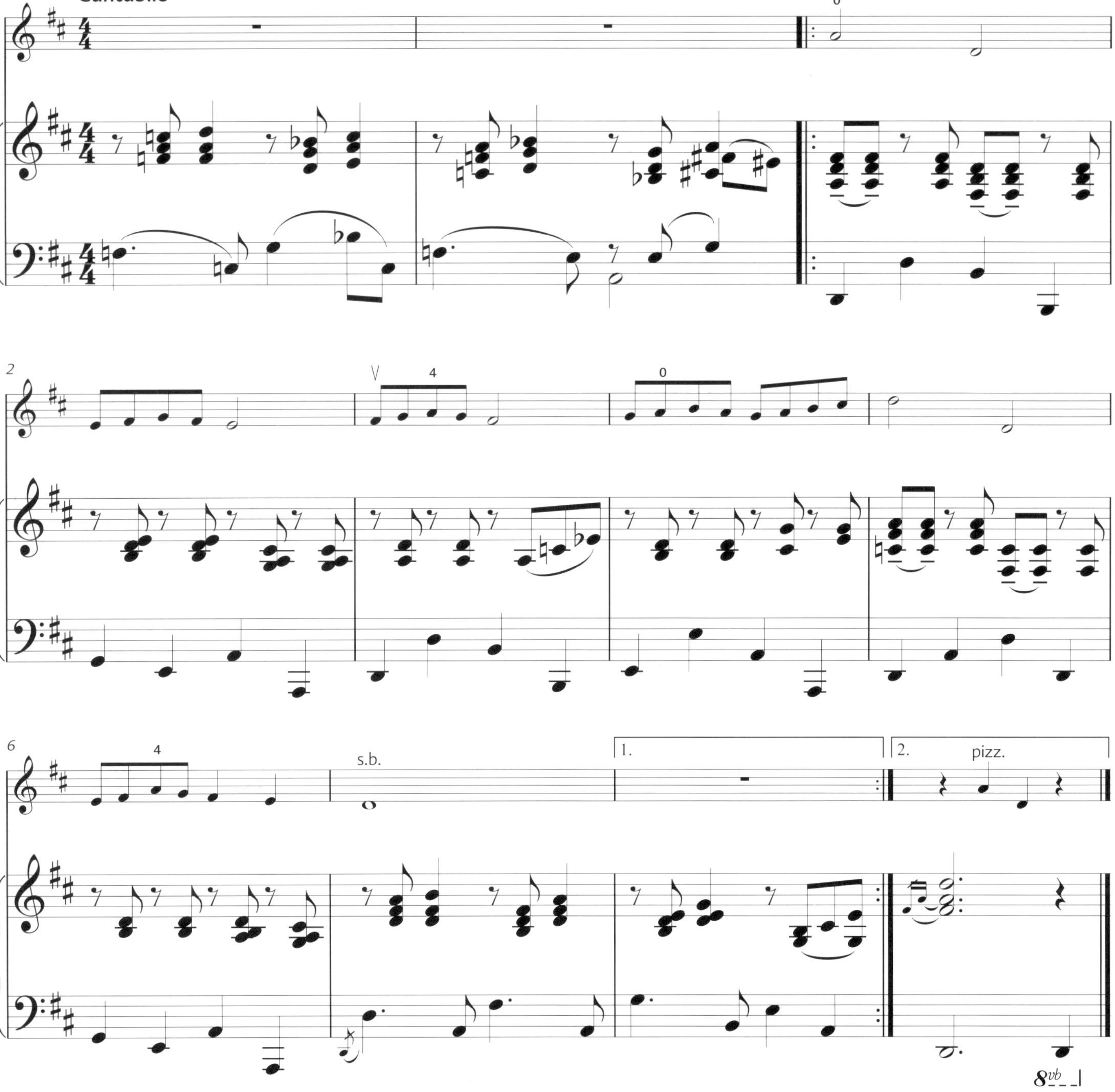
s.b.
1.
2.
pizz.
8vb

41 (Meet the) Flintstones

Joseph Barbera, William Hanna and Hoyt Curtin

With energy

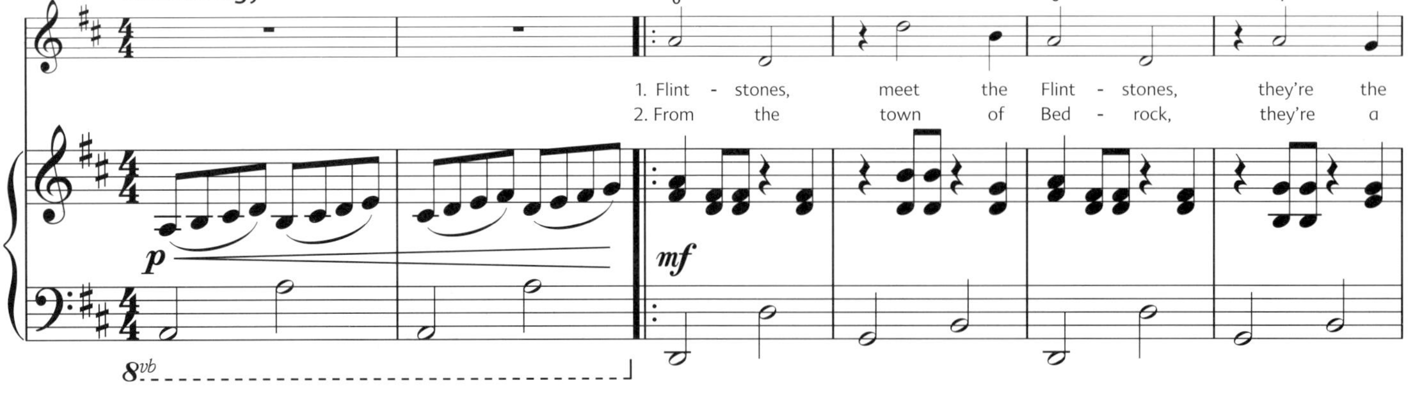
1. Flint - stones, meet the Flint - stones, they're the
2. From the town of Bed - rock, they're a
p
mf
8vb

42 I came from Alabama

traditional North American, arr. CH

43 Morningtown ride

Malvina Reynolds

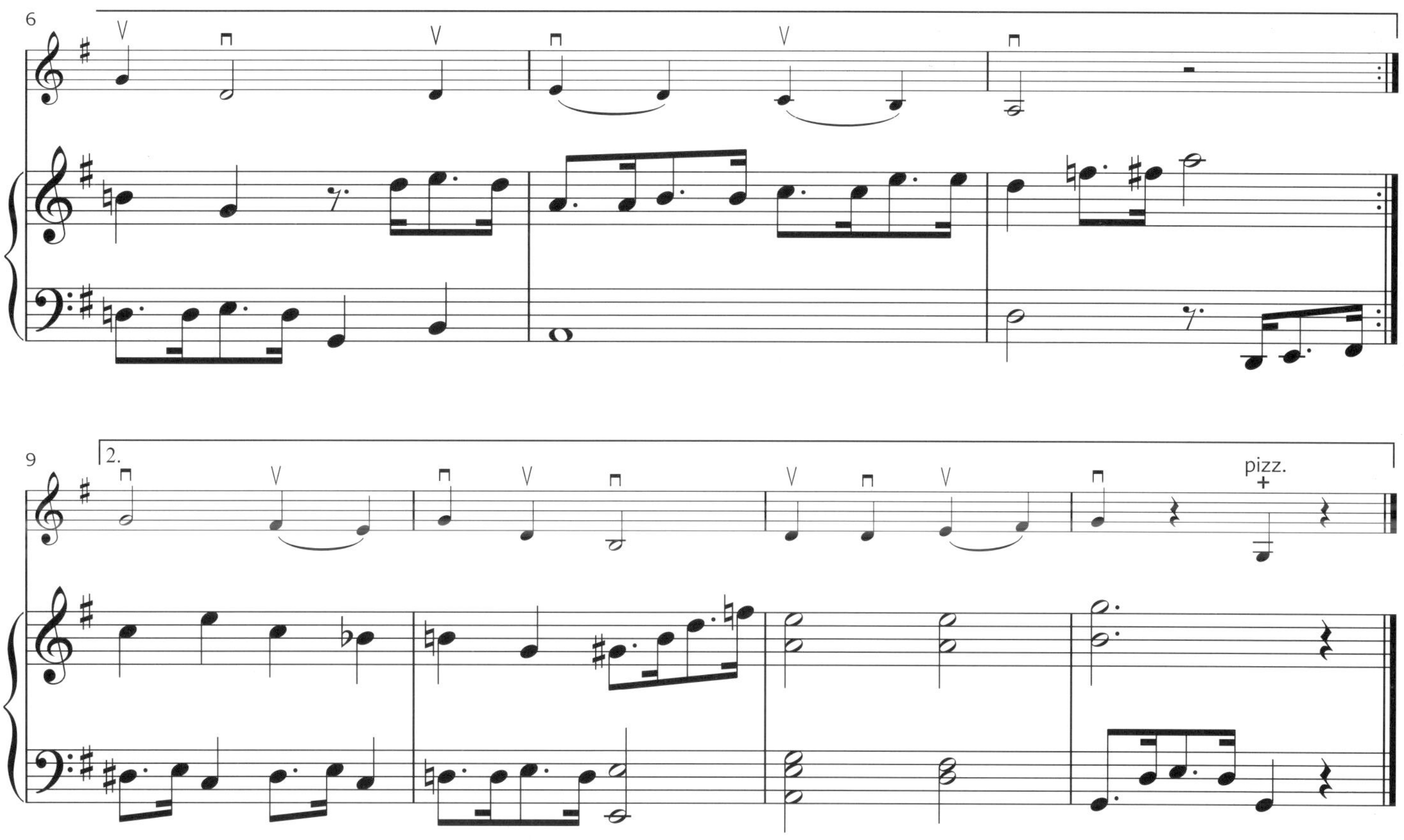
2.
pizz.

44 Troika

Serge Prokofieff

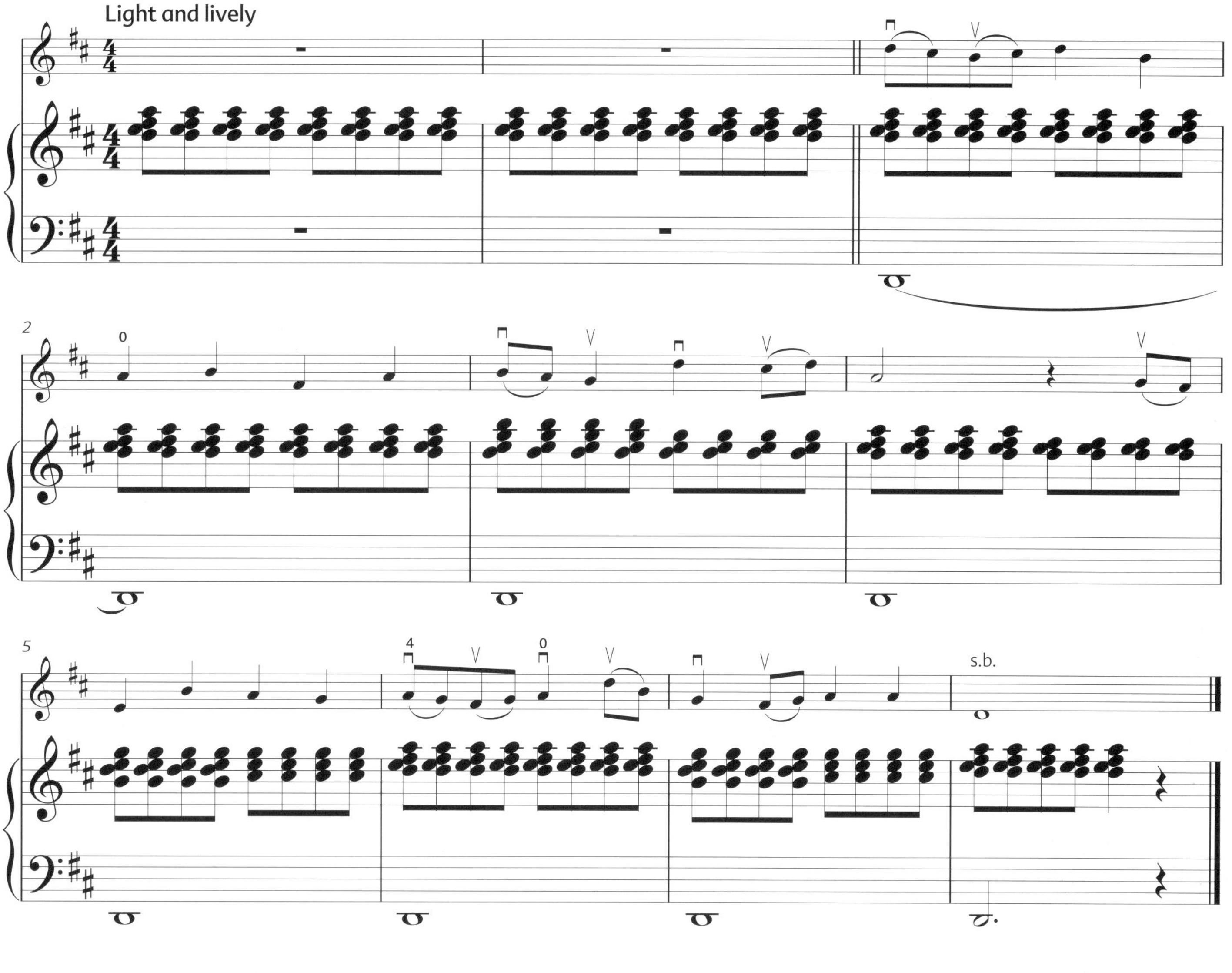
Light and lively
s.b.

45 Daydreamer

46 Roses from the South

Johann Strauss II

9
2.
pizz.

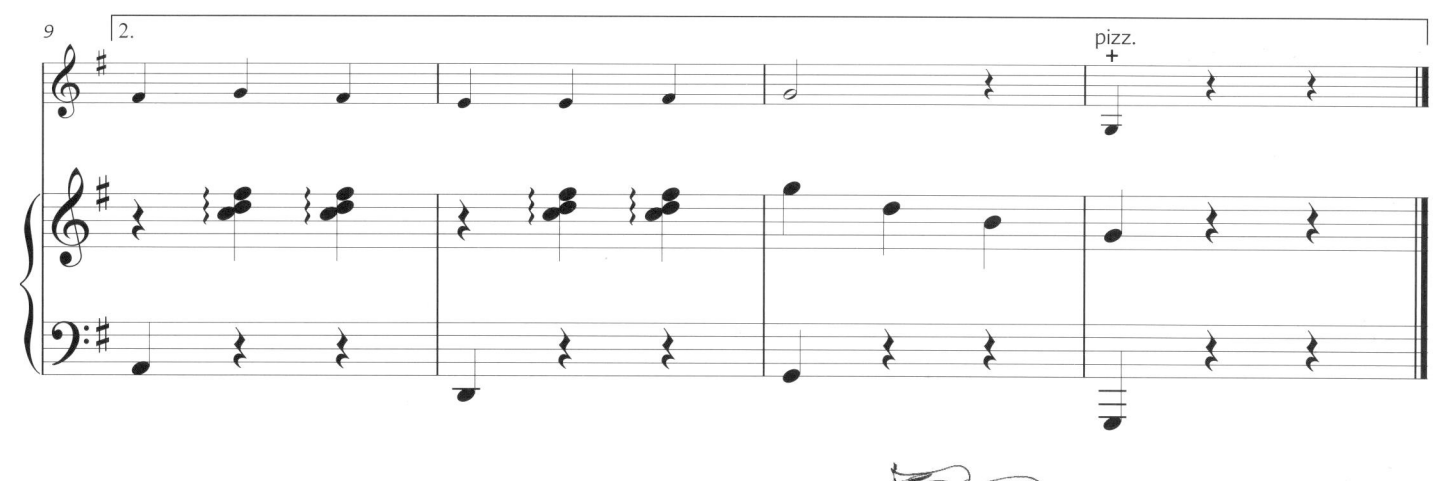

47 Lavender's blue

traditional

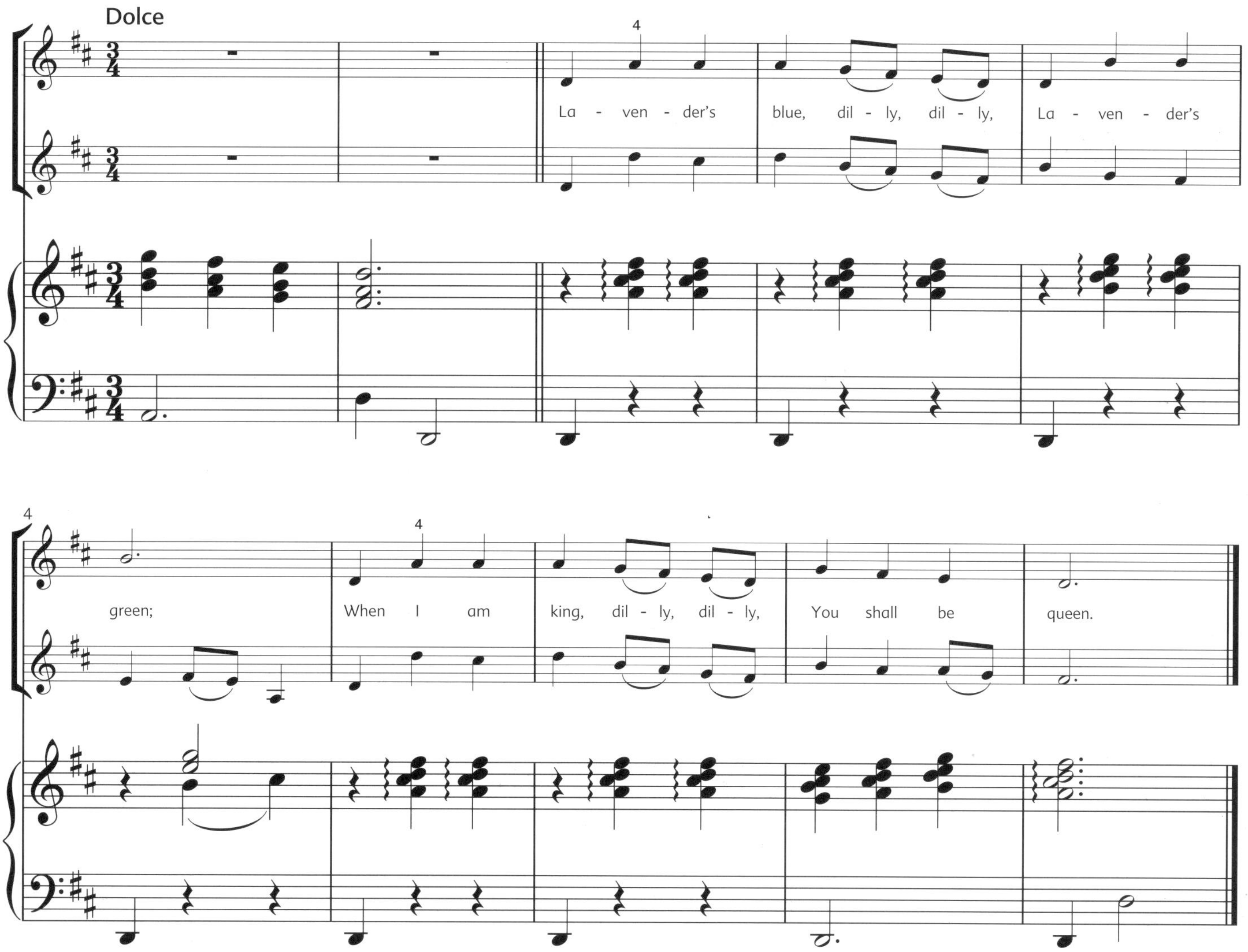
Dolce
4
La - ven - der's blue, dil - ly, dil - ly, La - ven - der's
4
green;
4
When I am king, dil - ly, dil - ly, You shall be queen.

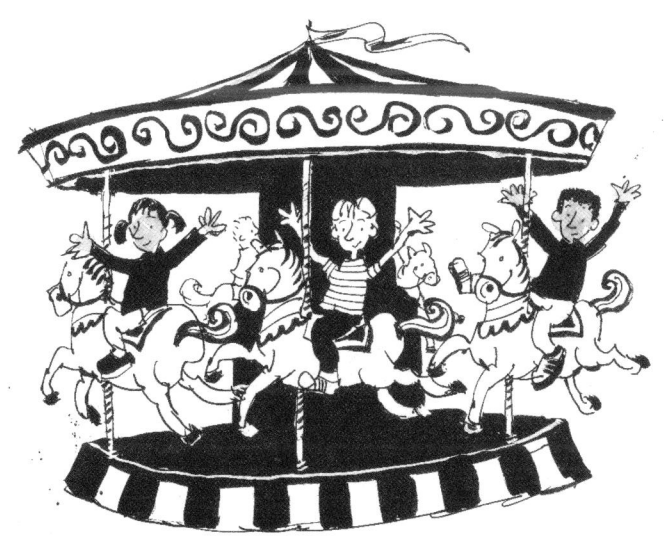

48 Call of the carousel

49 We all stand together

Paul McCartney

50 Edelweiss

words Oscar Hammerstein II, music Richard Rodgers

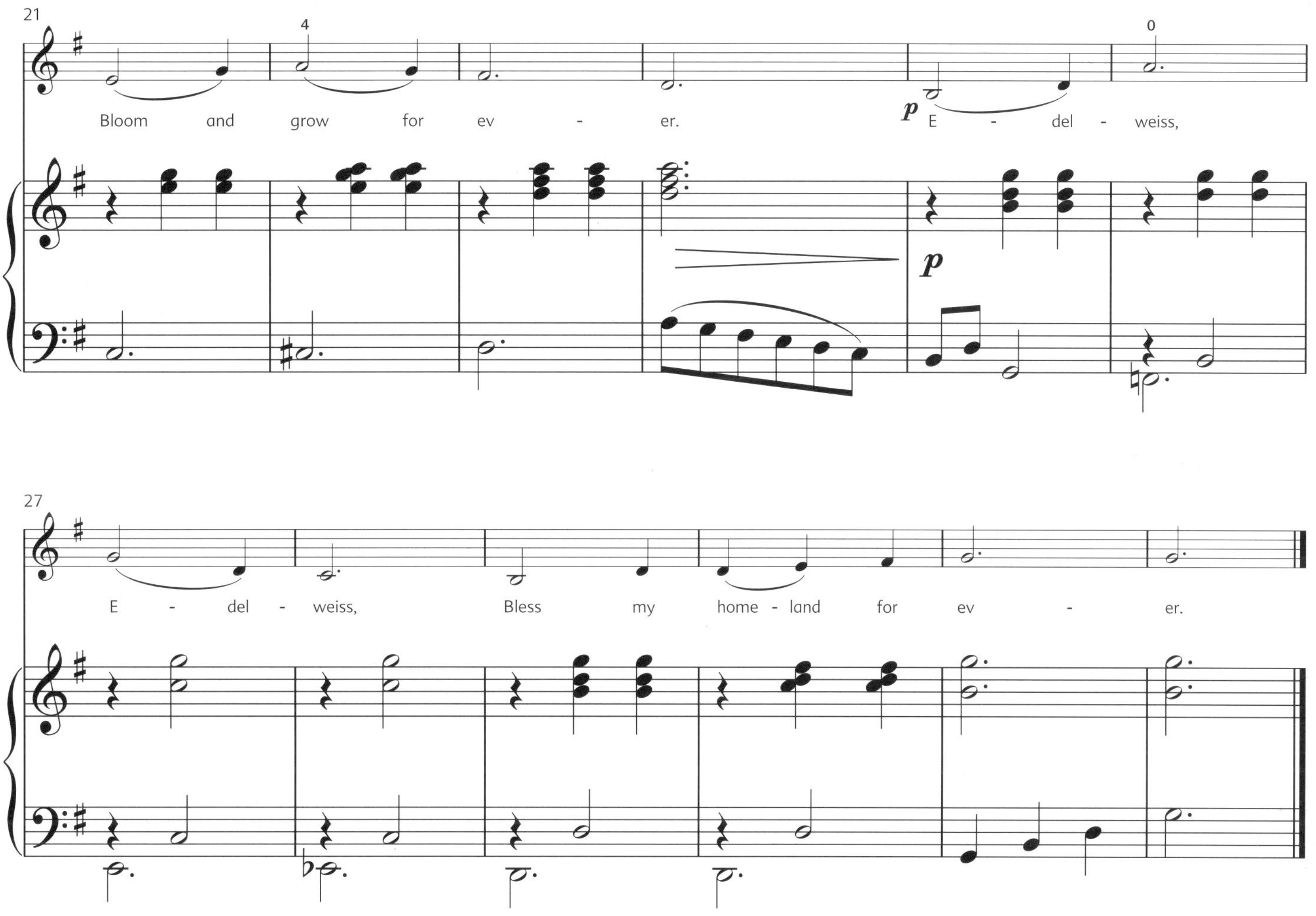
21
4
0
Bloom and grow for ev - er.
p E - del - weiss,
p
27
E - del - weiss,
Bless my home - land for ev - er.

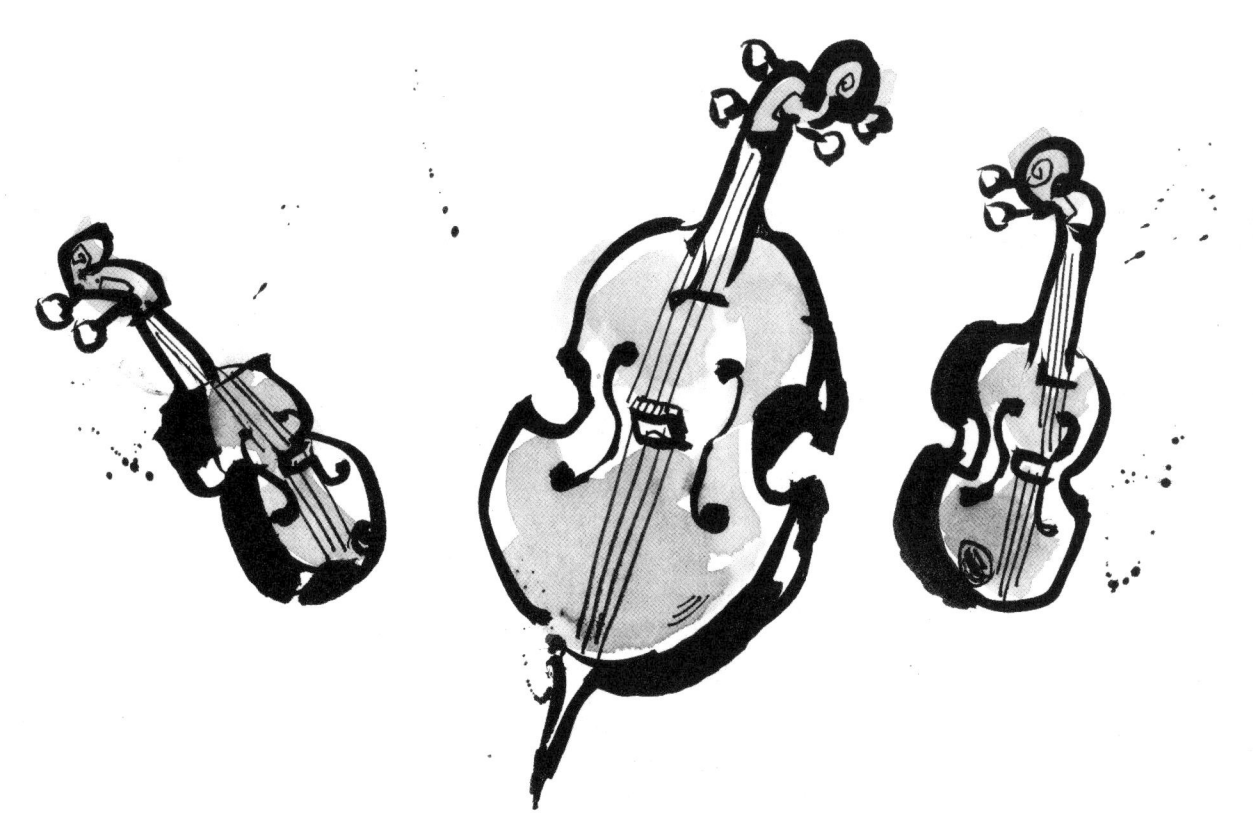

51 On top of Old Smokey

traditional North American

52 London's burning (a round)

traditional

Lon - don's burn - ing, Lon - don's burn - ing, Fetch the en - gines, fetch the en - gines, Fire, fire! Fire, fire! Pour on wa - ter, pour on wa - ter.

✶ entry point when played as a round

The accompaniment fits when the piece is played both as a solo and as a round — repeat the last two bars of accompaniment as necessary until the last player has finished.

53 The hippopotamus song

words Michael Flanders, music Donald Swann

54 London Bridge

traditional

55 Tea for two

words Irving Caesar, music Vincent Youmans, arr. CH

56 Stand by me

Ben E King, Jerry Leiber and Mike Stoller, arr. CH

Omit piano RH if teacher's instrumental part is played.

57 Skye boat song

traditional Scottish

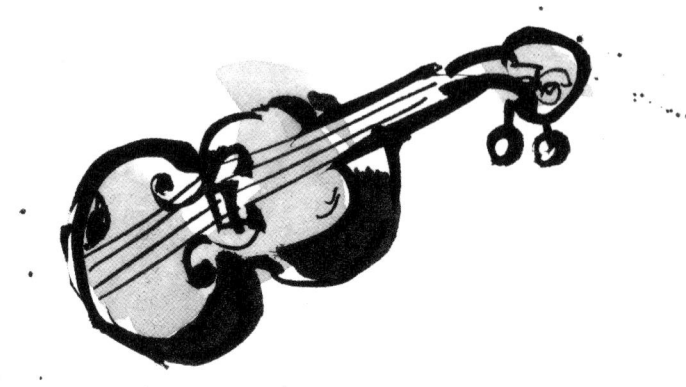

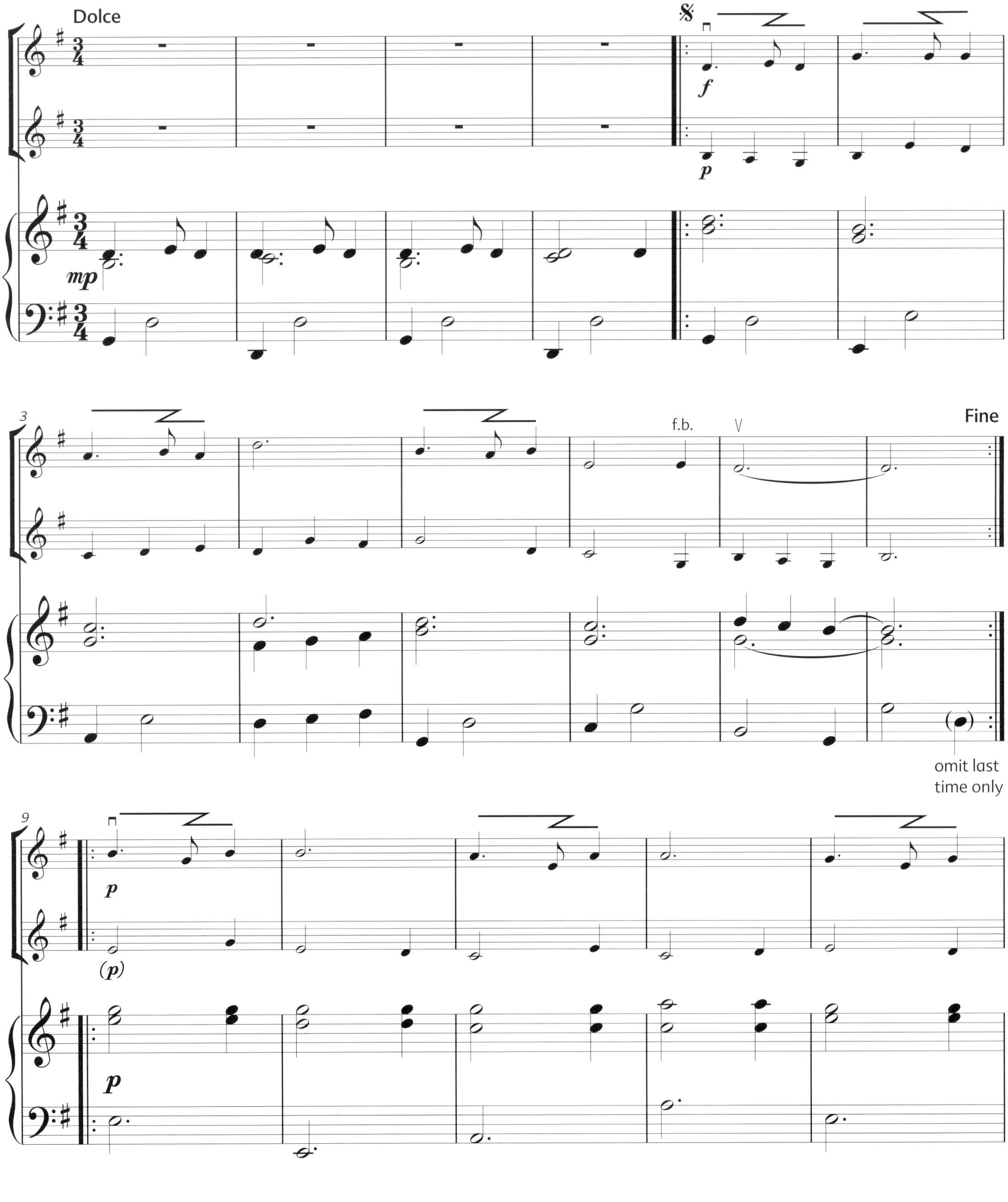
Dolce
mp
f
p
3
f.b.
Fine
omit last time only
9
p
(p)
p

Pupil's part written with D.C. al Fine instead of D.S. al Fine.

58 Jupiter

Gustav Holst

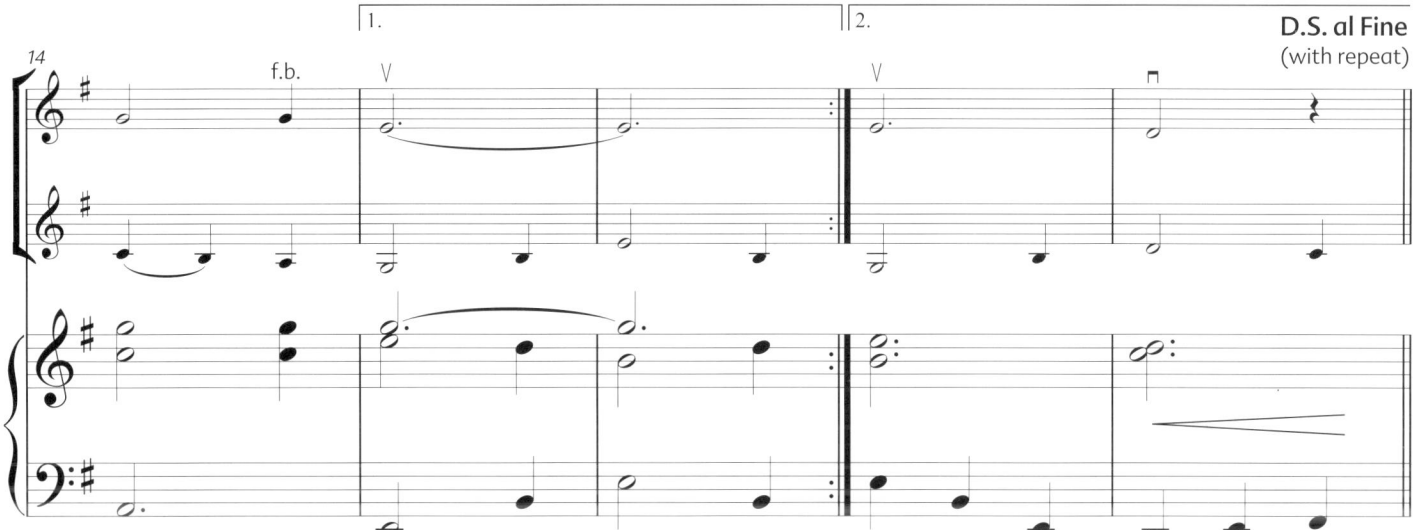

59 Feed the birds

Richard M Sherman and Robert B Sherman

60 Kalinka

traditional Russian

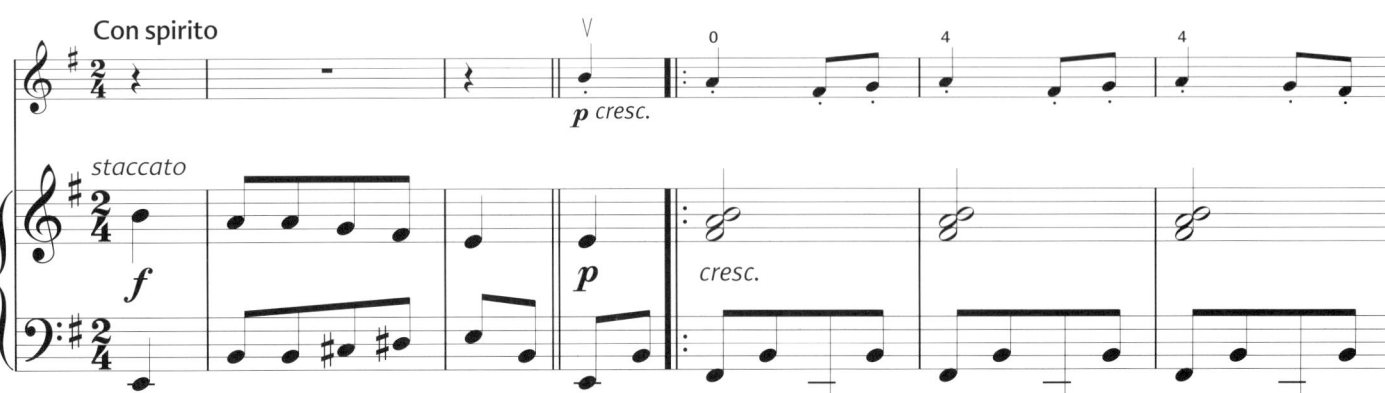

61 The old bazaar in Cairo

traditional

* entry point when played as a round

The accompaniment fits when the piece is played both as a solo and as a round — repeat the last eight bars of accompaniment as necessary until the last player has finished.

63 Waltz

Franz Lehar

64 Puff the magic dragon

Peter Yarrow and Leonard Upton

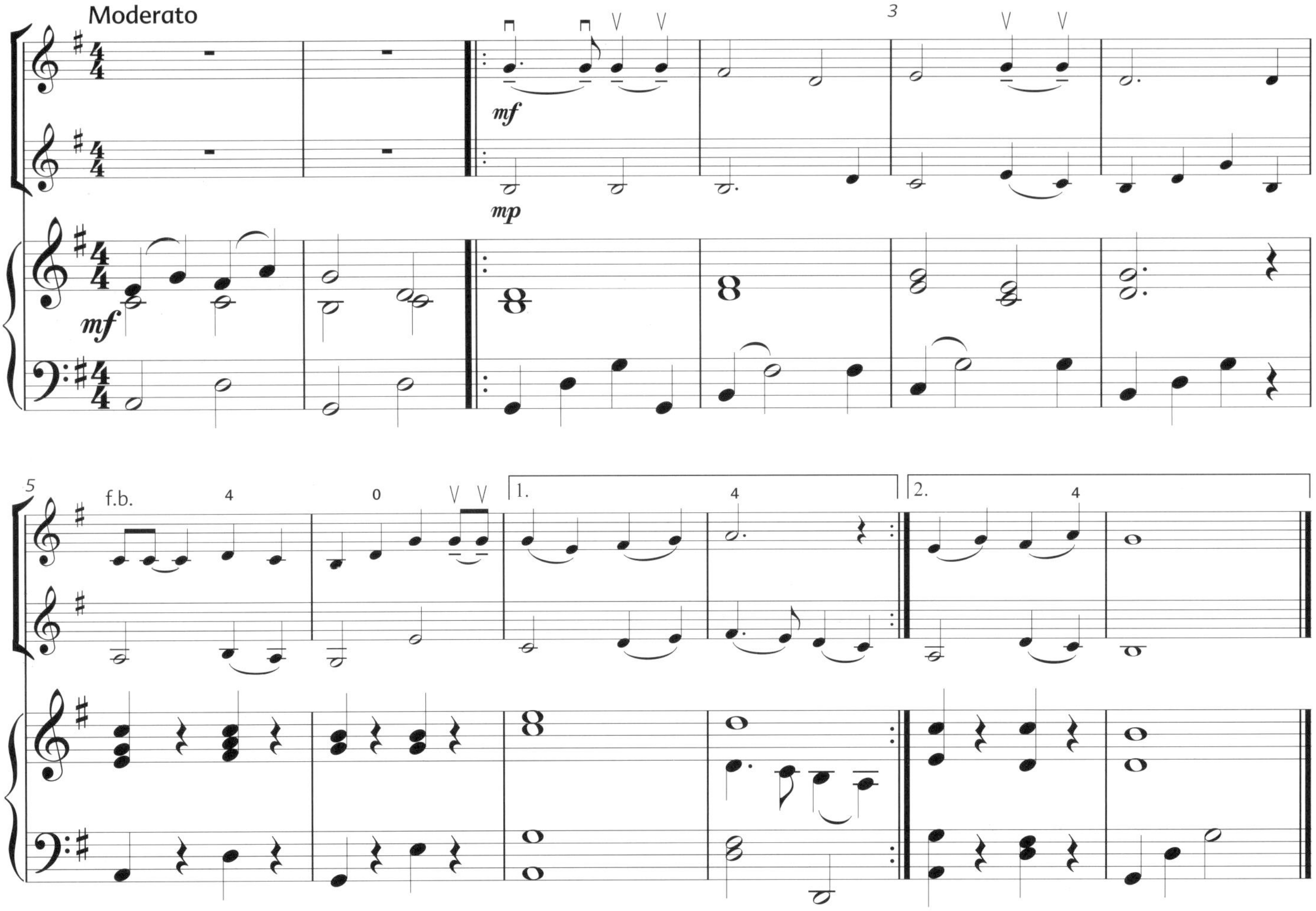

Moderato
f.b.

65 Dumplins

traditional Caribbean

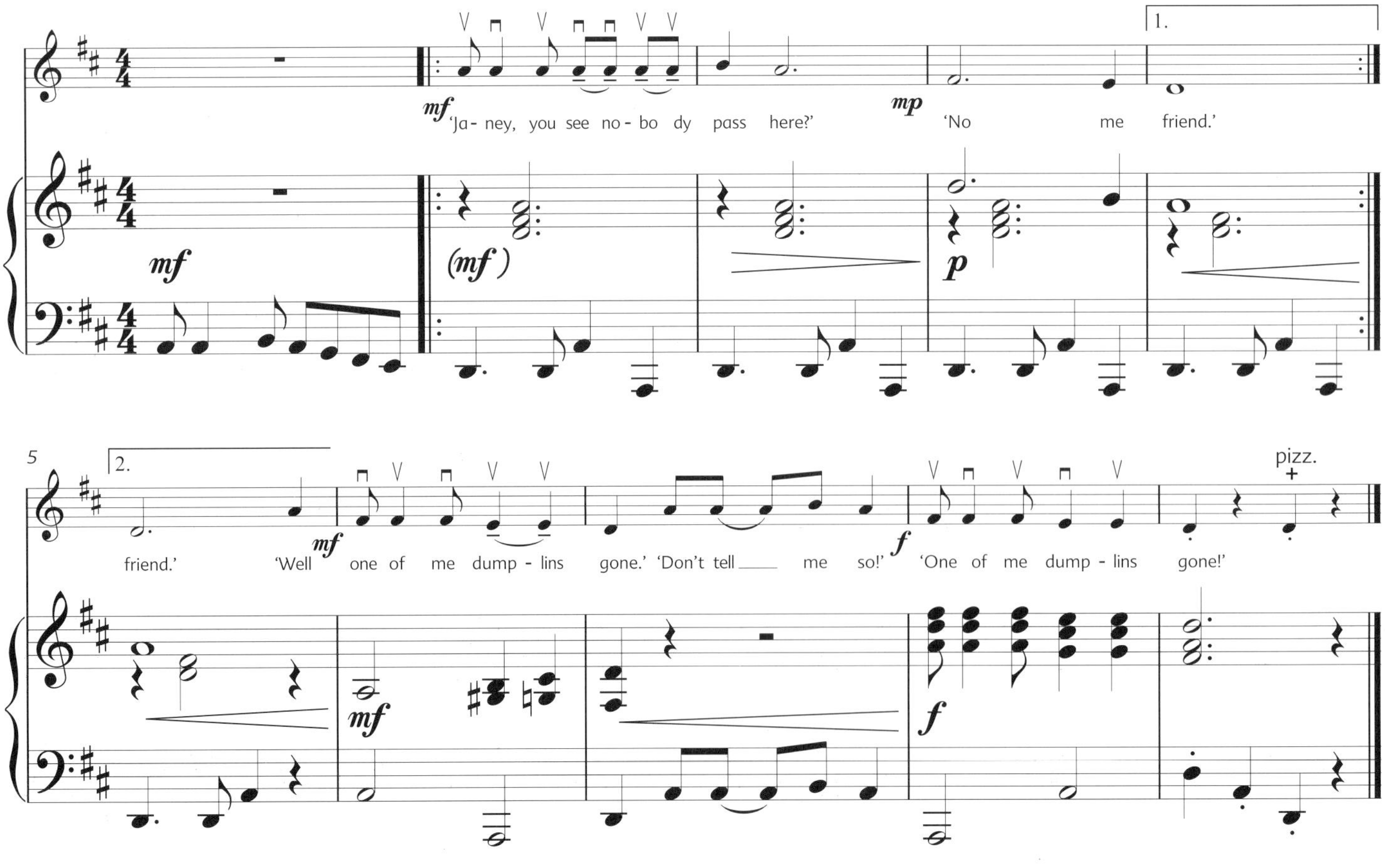

'Ja- ney, you see no- bo dy pass here?'
'No me friend.'
friend.'
'Well one of me dump - lins gone.'
'Don't tell me so!'
'One of me dump - lins gone!'
pizz.

66 Row, row, row your boat (a round)

traditional

∗ entry point when played as a round

The accompaniment fits when the piece is played both as a solo and as a round — repeat the last two bars of accompaniment as necessary until the last player has finished.

67 Pop! goes the weasel

traditional

70 We're off to see the Wizard

words E Y Harburg, music Harold Arlen

71 Egyptian snake dance

traditional

72 Shalom (a round)

traditional Israeli

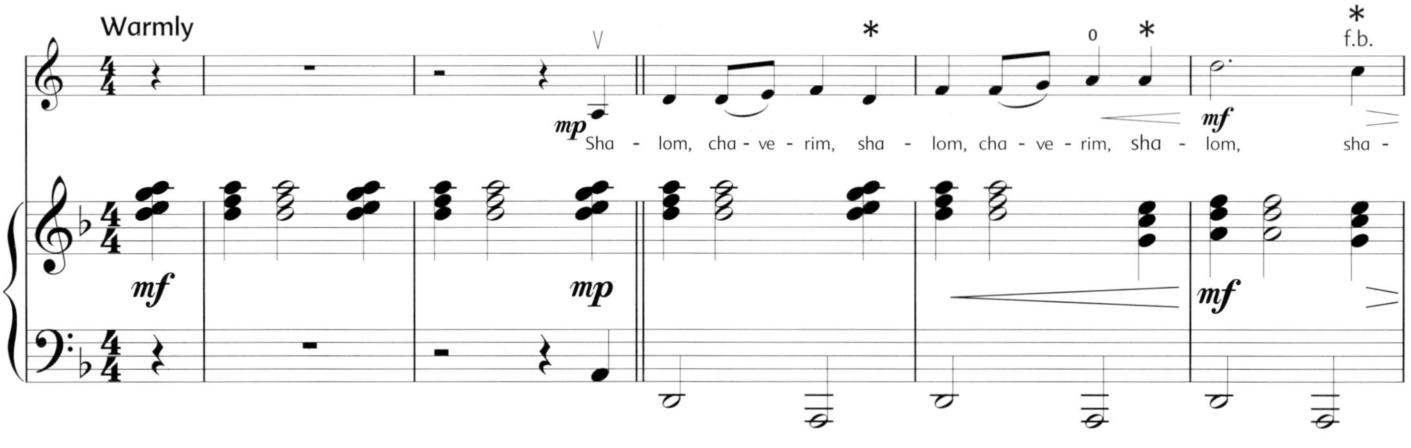

Sha - lom, cha - ve - rim, sha - lom, cha - ve - rim, sha - lom, sha -

4
f.b.
mp
-lom. Le - hi - tra - ot, le - hi - tra - ot, sha - lom, sha - lom.
p
mf
8vb

* entry point when played as a round

The accompaniment fits when the piece is played both as a solo and as a round — repeat the last bar of accompaniment as necessary until the last player has finished.

73 Summer is icumen in (a round)

traditional

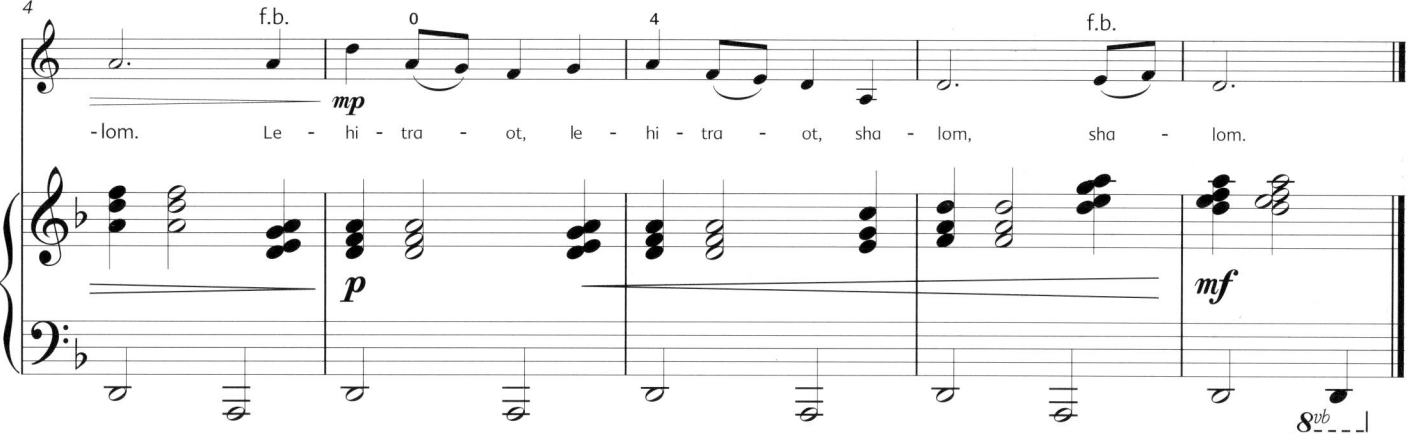

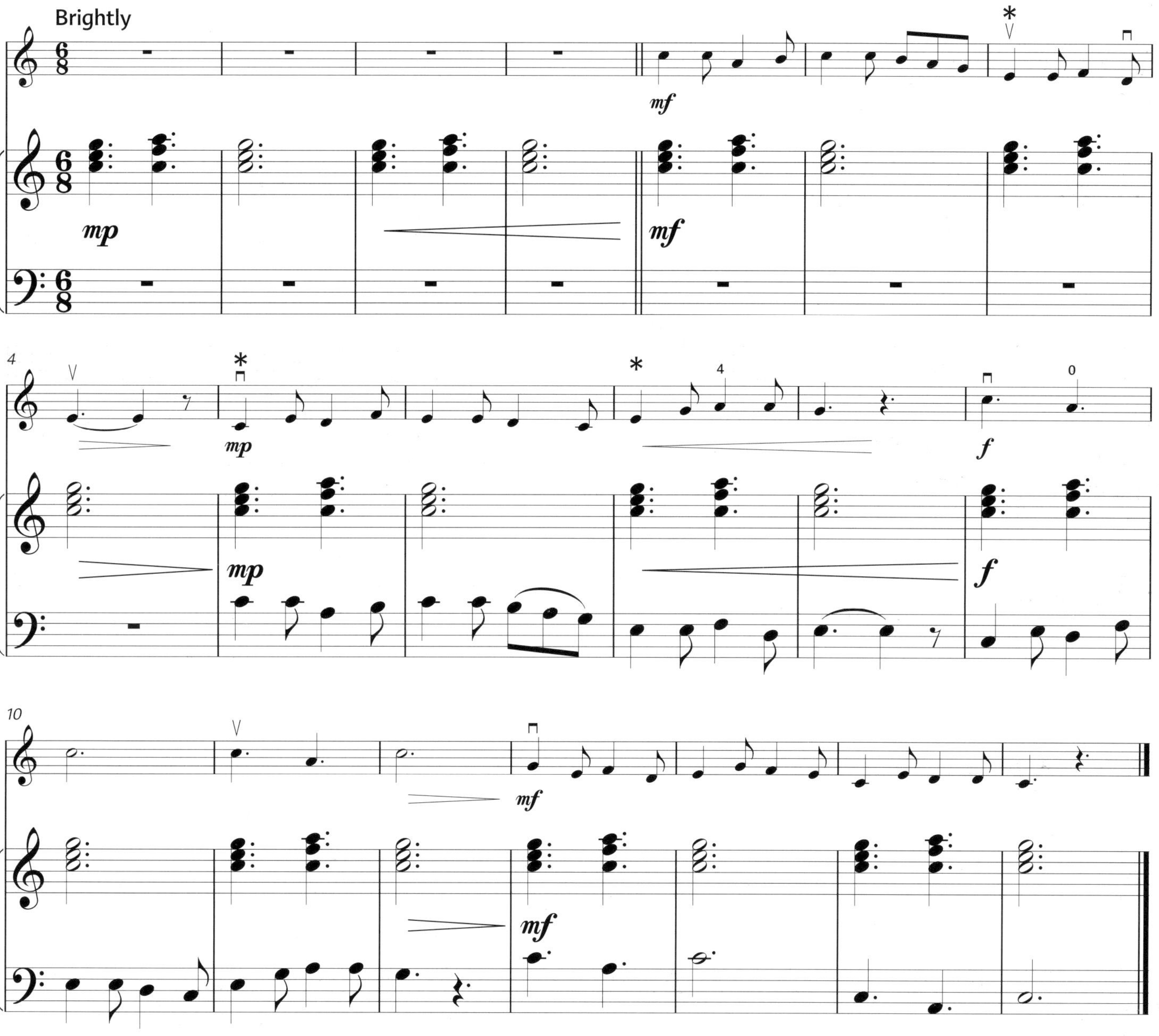

Brightly
mp
mf
4
mp
f
10
mf

* entry point when played as a round

The accompaniment fits when the piece is played both as a solo and as a round — repeat the last two bars of accompaniment as necessary until the last player has finished.

74 Part of your world

words Howard Ashman, music Alan Menken

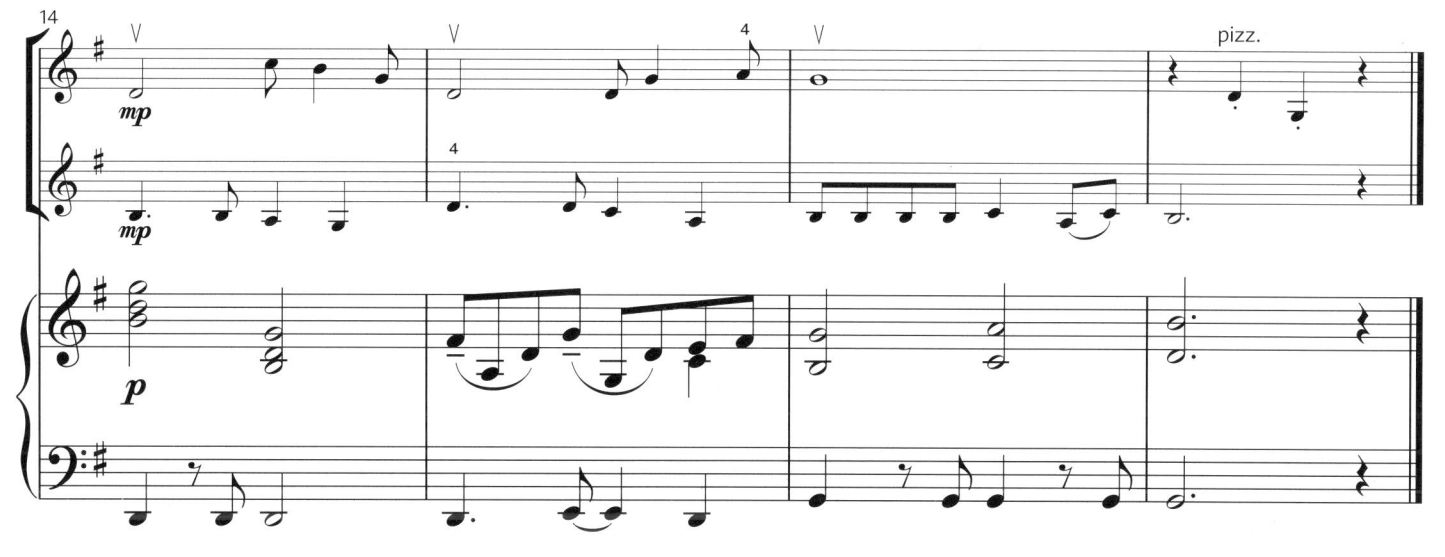

75 Short'nin' bread

Jacques Wolfe and Clement Wood

76 What shall we do with the drunken sailor?

traditional

77 Winter wonderland

words Richard Smith, music Felix Bernard

78 EastEnders

Leslie Osborne and Simon May

For a more authentic introduction, play:

79 Happy birthday

Patty S Hill and Mildred Hill

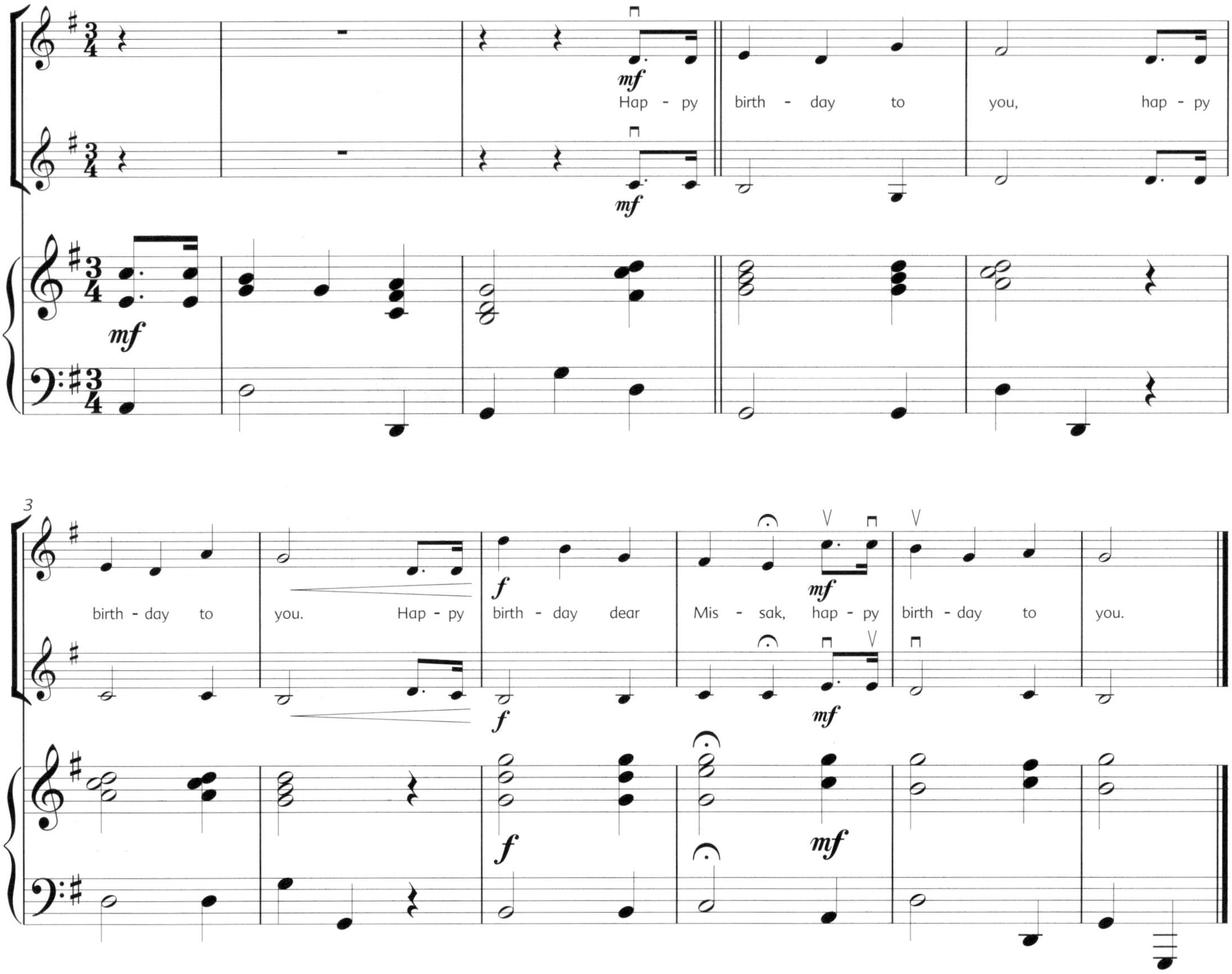

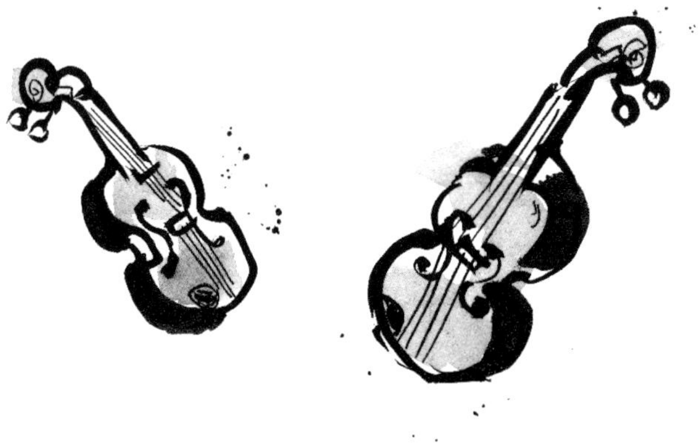

Hap - py birth - day to you, hap - py birth - day to you. Hap - py birth - day dear Mis - sak, hap - py birth - day to you.

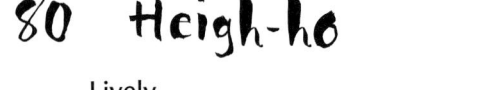

80 Heigh-ho

words Larry Morey, music Frank Churchill

Lively

'Heigh - ho', 'Heigh - ho', To make your trou - bles go, Just

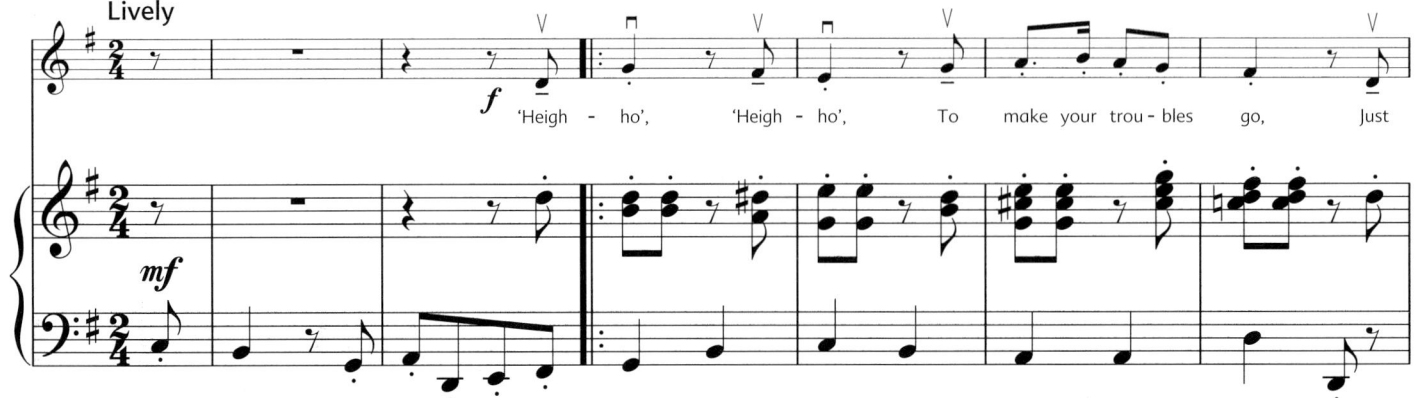

keep on sing - ing all day long 'Heigh - ho', 'Heigh - ho', 'Heigh - ho', 'Heigh - ho', 'Heigh - ho'.

81 The Addams family

Vic Mizzy

Spookily

Finger clicks

Finger clicks
Tongue clicks
Finger clicks
Tongue clicks
Finger clicks

82 The mocking bird

traditional Caribbean

Layout in pupil's part is different from above.

84 Ragamuffin's rag for violin

85 Who will buy? for violin, and for viola/cello playing the melody
Lionel Bart

Who will buy this wonderful morning? Such a sky you never did see! Who will tie it up with a ribbon, And put it in a box for me?

85. Who will buy? for viola/cello playing the accompaniment
Lionel Bart

87 Barcarolle

Jacques Offenbach

Tempo di valse

88 Millennium

Robert Williams, Guy Chambers, John Barry and Leslie Bricusse

89 Watch out kookaburra! (a round)

traditional Australian

Koo-ka-bur-ra sits on the te-le-phone wire, Watch out koo-ka-bur-ra's fea-thers on fire! Fly koo-ka-bur-ra, fly koo-ka-bur-ra, Flap your wings, fly high.

✳ entry point when played as a round

The accompaniment fits when the piece is played both as a solo and as a round — repeat the last two bars of accompaniment as necessary until the last player has finished.

90 Nocturne for violin

Aleksander Borodin

90 Nocturne for viola/cello

Aleksander Borodin

ACKNOWLEDGEMENTS

The author and publisher would like to thank the following for their help in the preparation of this book: Jeremy Birchall, Patricia Birchall, Jennifer Boston, Adrian Bradbury, Emily Brayshaw, Chris Bryant, Helen Crayford, Janet Crew, Peter Davey, Louise Dearsley, Tanya Demidova, Philip Dukes, Heather Fleck, David W Giles, Emily Haward, Jocelyn Lucas, Andrew Lynwood, Grace Lynwood, Barry Newland, Malcolm Pallant, Maja Passchier, Aoife Patarot-Hinds, Roland Roberts, Sheena Roberts, Valérie Saint-Pierre, Elaine Scott, Michelle Simpson, Holly Stirling, Dominic Viall, Matthew Watson and Allison Whitehead.

Very special thanks go to Carla Moss.

We are grateful to the following copyright owners who have kindly granted permission for the reprinting of these items:

Beauty and the beast Music by Alan Menken, words by Howard Ashman © 1991 Wonderland Music Company Inc/Walt Disney Music Company. Used by permission of Music Sales Ltd. All Rights Reserved. International Copyright secured;

Chim chim cher-ee Music and words by Richard M Sherman and Robert B Sherman © 1963 Wonderland Music Company Inc. Used by permission of Music Sales Ltd. All Rights Reserved. International Copyright Secured;

Dance of the cuckoos (Ku-ku) By T Marvin Hatley © 1930, 1932 Hatley Music Company, USA. Robert Kingston Music Limited, 8/9 Frith Street, London W1. Used by permission of Music Sales Ltd. All Rights Reserved. International Copyright Secured;

Eastenders by Leslie Osborne & Simon May © 1985 ATV Music. Sony/ATV Music Publishing (UK) Limited, 10 Great Marlborough Street, London W1. Used by permission of Music Sales Ltd. All Rights Reserved. International Copyright Secured;

Edelweiss from the Sound of Music. Words by Oscar Hammerstein II, music by Richard Rodgers © 1959 by Richard Rodgers and Oscar Hammerstein II. Copyright renewed. This arrangement © 2002 by Williamson Music. Williamson Music owner of publication and allied rights throughout the world. International Copyright Secured. All Rights Reserved;

Feed the birds Music and words by Richard M Sherman and Robert B Sherman © 1963 Wonderland Music Company Inc. Used by permission of Music Sales Ltd. All Rights Reserved. International Copyright Secured;

Halfway down the stairs Text by A A Milne and music by H Fraser Simson. Copyright under the Berne Convention;

Happy birthday to you Words and music by Patty S Hill and Mildred Hill © 1935 Summy Birchard Inc, USA. Keith Prowse Music Publishing Co Ltd, London WC2H OQY (for Europe) and Warner/Chappell Ltd, London W6 8BS (for World excl Europe);

Heigh ho Words by Larry Morey. Music by Frank Churchill © copyright 1938 by Bourne Co. Copyright Renewed. This arrangement © copyright 2002 by Bourne Co. All Rights Reserved. International Copyright Secured. Printed with permission from Bourne Music Ltd;

Lieutenant Kijé (Troika) by Prokofieff. Copyright © 1936 by Boosey & Co Ltd. Reproduced by permission of Boosey & Hawkes Music Publishers Ltd;

(Meet the) Flintstones Words and music by Joseph Barbera, William Hanna and Hoyt Curtin © 1960, 1962 (renewed) Barbara-Hanna Music, USA. Warner/Chappell Music Ltd London W6 8BS. Reproduced by permission of International Music Publications Ltd. All Rights Reserved. The Flintstones ™ is a trademark of and copyrighted by Hanna-Barbera Productions Inc;

Millennium Words and music by Robert Williams, Guy Chambers, John Barry and Leslie Bricusse © 1998 EMI Virgin Music Ltd, BMG Music Publishing Ltd and EMI United Partnership Ltd, USA. (33.33%) Worldwide print rights controlled by Warner Bros. Publications Inc/IMP Ltd. All Rights Reserved. (This song contains a sample of YOU ONLY LIVE TWICE by John Barry and Leslie Bricusse © EMI United Partnership Ltd.) Used by permission of Music Sales Ltd and International Music Publications. All Rights Reserved. International Copyright Secured;

Morningtown ride © 1959 by Amadeo Brio Music Inc. Administered by MCS Music Ltd, 32 Lexington Street, London W1F OLQ;

Off to France in the morning, One finger dance, Spinning wheel, Summer shine and **Windmill song** © 1985 Peter Davey;

Part of your world Music by Alan Menken, words by Howard Ashman © 1988 Wonderland Music Company Inc/Walt Disney Music Company. Used by permission of Music Sales Ltd. All Rights Reserved. International Copyright Secured.

Puff the magic dragon Words and music by Lenny Lipton and Peter Yarrow. Copyright © 1963; renewed 1991 Honalee Melodies (ASCAP) and Silver Dawn Music (ASCAP). Worldwide rights for Honalee Melodies administered by Cherry Lane Music Publishing Inc. Worldwide rights for Silver Dawn Music administered by WB Music Corp. 70% Warner/chappell Music Limited, London W6 8BS. 30% Cherry Lane Music Publishing Inc. All Rights Reserved. International copyright secured;

Short'nin' bread © Copyright 1928 (renewed) by Harold Flammer Music (ASCAP), a division of Shawnee Press Inc. International Copyright Secured. All Rights Reserved. Reproduced by permission of Chester Music Limited;

Stand by me Words and music by Ben E King, Jerry Leiber and Mike Stoller © 1961 (renewed) Jerry Leiber Music, Mike Stoller Music and Trio Music Company INC. This arrangement © 2002 Jerry Leiber Music, Mike Stoller Music and Trio Music Company INC. All Rights Reserved;

Supercalifragilisticexpialidocious Music and words by Richard M Sherman and Robert B Sherman. Used by permission of Music Sales Ltd. All Rights Reserved. International Copyright Secured;

Tea For two Words by Irving Caesar, music by Vincent Youmans © 1920 Harms Inc, USA Warner/Chappell Music Ltd, London W6 8BS. Reproduced by permission of International Music Publications Ltd. All Rights Reserved;

The Addams family Words and music by Vic Mizzy © 1964 Unison Music, USA. EMI Music Publishing Ltd, London, WC2H OQY. Reproduced by permission of International Music Publications Ltd. All Rights Reserved. Europe only;

The hippopotamus song Words by Michael Flanders, music by Donald Swann © 1952 Chappell Music Ltd, London W6 8BS. Reproduced by permission of International Music Publications Ltd. All Rights Reserved;

The way you look tonight Music by Jerome Kern, words by Dorothy Fields © 1936 T B Harms & Company Inc, USA and Jerome Kern. 50% Warner Chappell Music Limited, Griffin House 161 Hammersmith Road, London W6 (50%)/Polygram Music Publishing Limited, 47 British Grove, London W4 (50%). Used by permission of Music Sales Ltd and International Music Publications Limited. All Rights Reserved. International Copyright Secured;

Theme from Jupiter from The Planets Op 32 Music by Gustav Holst © copyright 1921 Goodwin & Tabb Limited. Transferred to J Curwen & Sons Limited, 8/9 Frith Street, London W1D 3JB. All Rights Reserved. Reproduced by permission;

Waltz from **The merry widow** Original words by Leo Stein and Viktor Leon. English translation by Adrian Ross. Music by Franz Lehar. © 1964 Glocken Verlag Ltd. Chappell Music Ltd, London W6 8BS. Reproduced by permission of International Music Publications Limited. All rights reserved;

We all stand together Words and music by Paul McCartney © 1984 MPL Communications Ltd;

We're off to see the wizard Words by E Y Harburg, music by Harold Arlen © 1939 EMI Catalogue Partnership, EMI Feist Catalog Inc and EMI United Partnership Ltd, USA. Worldwide print rights controlled by Warner Bros. Publications Inc/IMP Ltd. Reproduced by permission of International Music Publications Ltd. All Rights Reserved;

Whistle while you work Words by Larry Morey. Music by Frank Churchill. © copyright 1937 by Bourne Co. All Rights Reserved. International Copyright Secured. Printed with permission from Bourne Music Ltd;

Who will buy? © 1960 Lakeview Music Publishing Co Ltd. Suite 2.07, Plaza 535 Kings Road, London SW10 0SZ. International Copyright Secured. All Rights Reserved. Used by permission;

Winter wonderland Words by Richard Smith, music by Felix Bernard © 1934 Bregman Vocco & Conn Inc, USA. (50%) Francis Day & Hunter Ltd, London WC2H OQY (50%) Redwood Music Ltd, London NW1 8BD. Reproduced by permission of International Music Publications Ltd. Europe only.

All other original pieces and arrangements are copyright A&C Black.

Every effort has been made to trace and acknowledge copyright owners. If any right has been omitted, the publishers offer their apologies and will rectify this in subsequent editions following notification.